BOOTS & WISHES

UGLY STICK SALOON SERIES BOOK #10

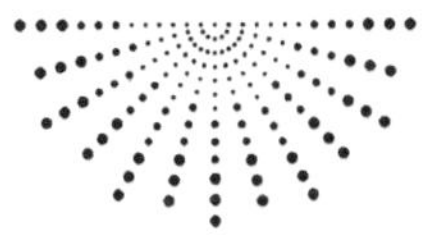

MYLA JACKSON

TWISTED PAGE INC

BOOTS & WISHES

UGLY STICK SALOON SERIES BOOK #10

New York Times & *USA Today*
Bestselling Author

ELLE JAMES

writing as

MYLA JACKSON

This book is dedicated to couples who have struggled to get pregnant, the heartache that comes when it doesn't happen right away, and the ultimate joy of discovering you can and will have a baby.

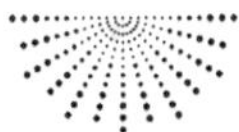

CHAPTER ONE

"Hey, cowboy, what say you strap on the chaps and we go for a ride?" Audrey stood in the doorway of the storeroom, wearing chaps over her blue jean cutoffs and carrying a leather whip coiled in one hand. In her other hand was a pair of man-sized leather chaps. They were the ones out of his closet from home. She liked him best in the real deal.

Jackson's eyes widened and he teetered, almost losing his balance on the ladder he had climbed up to change the bulb in the fluorescent light fixture hugging the ceiling. He held the long white tube he'd been about to install in the slot he'd just pulled the burned-out bulb from. "Now? Are you ovulating?"

"Do I have to be ovulating for you to want to make love to me?" Audrey's gut instantly knotted and her eyes stung. "Six months ago, you'd have dropped the bulb and leaped off the ladder at an offer like this." Her shoulders sagged and she sighed. "I was afraid of this."

Jackson set the new bulb in the slots and climbed down from the ladder. "Afraid of what?" He pulled her into his arms and kissed her forehead.

"Afraid making love would become a chore."

Jackson snorted. "Never."

"Admit it." She poked a finger at his chest. "Ever since we decided to try to get pregnant, we've lost some of the magic and spontaneity we used to enjoy."

When Jackson started to shake his head, Audrey raised her eyebrows and gave him a pointed look. "Be honest."

Jackson's head stopped in midshake and he grimaced. "Okay, so it's not quite as spontaneous as it used to be. But I love you and never get tired of making love with you."

"And I never tire of making love with you. But all the effort of timing our lovemaking is taking the joy out of our sex life." She stepped back and turned away from him, her heart sore. "Maybe we should give up trying. If it happens, it happens." She bit her bottom lip before continuing softly, "And if it doesn't, it wasn't meant to be. We weren't meant to be parents. I mean, my life has been anything but role-model material."

Warm, work-roughened hands curled around her arms and she was pulled back against Jackson's solid chest. "Sweetheart, it will happen. Most likely when we least expect it. And even if it doesn't—which I'm not giving up—you would be enough to keep me happy for the rest of my life. And you're the best role model a kid could have. You're real, tender-hearted, and you care about everyone you come in contact with."

Audrey's heart filled to overflowing. Jackson was the man who made her life complete. Her one true love. He loved her even with her background as a stripper. She couldn't imagine loving anyone else or living without him. She covered his hands on her arms and leaned back against him. "I love you, Jackson Gray Wolf. That will never change." Turning in his embrace, she cupped his cheek. His face was so dear to her and made her grateful every day of her life she'd found him. "I want to have your children. I want to see little Gray Wolf boys running around the ranch, learning to ride horses, swimming in the creek and raising hell like I'm certain you and your brothers did when you were growing up."

"And I want half a dozen little girls with strawberry-blond hair and eyes so blue they make the Texas skies pale in comparison."

"Nice." She slid her hands up his chest to lock behind his neck. "When did you become a romantic?"

"When I met you." He kissed her, his tongue sliding along the seam of her lips.

She parted her lips and teeth to him and his tongue, enjoying the way he stroked her, like having sex with their mouths. The man was everything a woman could want and more.

Tall, dark and handsome, with the high cheekbones and inky black eyes of his Kiowa ancestry. Dressed in jeans and a blue chambray shirt, he was a sexy mix of cowboy and Indian all wrapped up in a muscular package Audrey couldn't get enough of.

Her core tightened, her body warmed and she

backed away until her hand connected with the storeroom door. With a quick twist, she locked the door.

Jackson's eyes flared and a smile tilted the corners of his lips. He reached for his belt buckle and flicked it open.

"Now you're getting the right idea," Audrey purred. She handed him the leather chaps and paused to cup the bulge growing behind his fly.

While Jackson tied the chaps around his hips, Audrey yanked her tank top up over her breasts and tossed it onto a case of whiskey. "I thought I'd have to dance a striptease for you to get you excited."

"Sweetheart, all you have to do is stand there and I'm as hard as a steel rod." He stalked her, his fingers making quick work of the buttons on his jeans, popping them free one at a time.

Audrey jerked her zipper open and slipped her shorts down her legs. Wearing nothing but her bra, red cowboy boots and chaps, her pussy creamed and she couldn't wait to mount her cowboy and ride him until they both came.

Her sexy husband scooped her up by the backs of her thighs.

She wrapped her legs around his waist and eased down over his rock-hard cock. "Mmmm. Now that's what I'm talking about."

Jackson backed her against the door and pinned her hands above her head in one of his big ones. "Soft and sweet, or make it rough?" he asked.

"Ride me, baby," she breathed, her pulse pounding, a

wash of juices easing his thickness inside her. "Make it hard and fast. I'm already teetering on the edge."

"I aim to please." He braced her against the wood door and drove into her deep, long and hard, pulled out and thrust into her again. In and out, he moved, his hips pumping, his cock thickening with every stroke.

He filled her so tightly she couldn't think of anything else but him and the way he made her feel.

The tension built, her body tightened around him, and her breasts beaded, her blood flowing hot through her veins as she climbed that exquisite path to release.

The tingling began at her core and spread outward as she climaxed. Then Audrey was riding the waves of her orgasm, her body shuddering deliciously.

Jackson thrust one last time, burying himself deep inside her. He released his hold on her wrists, gripped her hips in his big hands and held her, his body rigid, his member full and throbbing against the walls of her channel.

When he finally relaxed and bent to capture her lips with his, he whispered, "I'll never get tired of this."

"Me either."

A loud banging on the door made Audrey jump.

"Hey, we're about out of longnecks up front. Could you guys stop boinking long enough for us to serve the customers?" Charli Sutton, Audrey's assistant manager, knocked again. "I know you're in there."

"I'll be out in a minute," Audrey called out. "With the longnecks." Audrey sighed and gathered her clothing. "Sometimes I wish I'd never bought the Ugly Stick."

Before she could slip her shirt over her shoulders,

Jackson pulled her against him and tweaked a beaded nipple. "Then we might never have met. This place brought us together. In fact, if not for this place, you wouldn't have hired Libby. Who knows what manner of woman Mark and Luke would have ended up with?"

Audrey smiled. "They do love each other, don't they? I've never seen Libby happier. And her father is finally beginning to accept that Mark and Luke both are part of her life."

"You've done so much for everyone who has ever come through those doors, including me." Jackson smoothed the hair off her brow. "You know the most beautiful thing about you?"

"No, but I have a feeling you're going to tell me." Audrey's heart swelled at the love in Jackson's eyes.

"Sure, your breasts are luscious and ripe for the tasting. The swell of your hips makes me hard all over again. And your eyes are so blue...well, I could get lost in them."

"Go on," she encouraged, her cup overflowing with his love.

Jackson gathered her close and tipped her chin up, lowering his mouth to hover over hers. "It's your heart that makes you so beautiful. You have so much love, empathy and compassion for others that everyone you meet falls in love with you."

"But I only love you," she said, her breath mingling with his. "The woman-loves-a-man kind of lov—"

Jackson stole her words away with a kiss, and Audrey forgot what she was saying and gave in to the temptation that was Jackson.

When he allowed her up for air, she leaned her forehead against his chest. "Even if we never have a baby, I'll be content as long as I have you."

"Content?" Jackson chuckled. "That doesn't sound inspiring." He helped her slip her tank top over her head, pinching the tip of one nipple through the lace of her bra. "I hope you'll be more than content. Hmmm." He bent to hold her shorts for her, helping her slide them up her legs and button them, his rough fingers skimming the sensitive skin over her tummy. "I'll have to work on that. Next thing you know, you'll be sliding into comfortable and we'll be sitting in rocking chairs, trying to remember where we left our teeth."

Audrey laughed and buttoned his jeans for him. "I'd be perfectly happy to grow old with you, Jackson Gray Wolf. Rocking chairs on the porch of the ranch house sounds like heaven. We could watch our grandchildren running around in the yard, playing tag."

"And our children would be sipping tea on the porch with us. All grown up and beautiful like their mother."

"You mean handsome like their father," Audrey corrected.

Jackson paused, his brow puckering. "Hey, hasn't it been two weeks since you last ovulated?"

"Two weeks and three days."

He glanced down at her belly. "And?"

Audrey chewed on her bottom lip. "I'm three days late for my period."

A smile spread across Jackson's face. "Why didn't you tell me?"

She shrugged. "I didn't want to get our hopes up."

"Is it too soon to take a pregnancy test?" he asked, buckling his belt. "Want me to go get one from the drug store?"

"The drug store is closed, sweetie. It closed four hours ago." Audrey touched his arm. "But I have one in my purse."

"Take it," he demanded. "Go, pee on it or do whatever it takes. I can't believe you haven't done it already."

Again, Audrey chewed on her bottom lip, her heart beating irregularly, alternating between the happy staccato of excitement and the dull thud of anticipated disappointment. "What if it comes out negative?"

"You don't know until you try."

"I wanted so much to be pregnant by Christmas."

"We've only just started trying. You have to be patient."

"Just started? It's been six months!"

"Half a year. It's nothing."

"It's five pregnancy tests and five negative results." A lump formed in Audrey's throat and she swallowed hard before continuing, "I don't know if I can stand another disappointment with Christmas so close."

Jackson pulled her into his arms again. "Christmas will be great, with or without a baby in your belly."

"But I wanted so much to be carrying your child by then." Her eyes welled and she fought to hold back the tears. No matter how hard she tried, one slipped out and trailed down her cheek.

"Oh, baby." Jackson brushed away the tear. "Trust me. Everything will work out. I promise."

"How can you promise something you might not be able to deliver?"

"You are worrying far too much. It's probably messing up your reproductive system. Relax." He shook her shoulders like a coach at a ball game. "It'll happen."

"Okay." She laughed. "I'll relax. And I'll try to make our 'sessions' more spontaneous."

"Right now, we'd better get those longnecks out front before the natives get restless and break down the door." Jackson hefted a case of beer and headed for the door.

Audrey unlocked it, leaned up to kiss Jackson's cheek and then opened the door. "I love you, babe."

He winked. "I love you more."

Audrey grabbed a couple of bottles of whiskey and followed Jackson through to the bar, enjoying the way his jeans rode his narrow hips. Oh yeah, making love to this hunk of a human was easy. What was harder was getting pregnant. She prayed she hadn't waited too long to start trying. Was thirty-two too old to get pregnant? She knew women who kept having babies well into their forties.

After Jackson settled the case of beer on the floor behind the bar, he kissed Audrey again and rounded the bar to join his brothers and friends at a table.

"I'll be glad when you two finally get pregnant." Charli bent over the case of longnecks and pulled several bottles out, loading them into the trough filled with ice to chill.

"You and me both." Audrey bent to grab three more,

handing them to Charli. "I don't know what we're doing wrong. I should be five months along by now."

"You can't expect to get pregnant on your first attempt, hon. It's not that exact a science."

"Okay, I didn't expect it on our first attempt, but we're five months into this and…" She waved a hand. "Nothing."

Charli straightened. "Oh, sweetie, this is really eating at you, isn't it?"

Audrey nodded, once again fighting the ready tears. "I never thought I'd ever want children. Until I met Jackson. Now I can't imagine not having children. Can't you just see them? All dark-haired, dark-eyed little boys running barefoot and wild?"

Shaking her head, Charli hugged her. "I *can* imagine. And you'll make a great mother, Audrey. You're like a mother to all of us misfits. It's about time you had a dozen children of your own, instead of playing momma to all of us."

Audrey smiled at Charli. The pretty blonde had been with her almost as long as Audrey had owned the bar. She wasn't just an employee. She was Audrey's best friend and confidant. "I know I've been very self-absorbed lately. How's it going for you? Have you set a date yet? When are you two going to tie the knot, settle down and have children?"

"Hey, this conversation isn't about me and Connor. It's about you, your man and the family you're trying to have."

"You haven't set a date, have you?" Audrey crossed

her arms. "Do I need to have a talk with Connor? Is he the hold-out?"

Charli's face flushed red. "Don't talk to Connor. He's more than ready to get married. I'm the hold-out."

Audrey's arms fell to her sides. "What's wrong? Have you two had an argument?"

Her assistant manager avoided answering by helping Libby serve several customers who'd come to the bar for refills on their beer mugs. When Charli returned to the case of beer, Audrey was waiting.

Charli shrugged. "I don't know. I just want to be sure before I make as big a commitment as marriage."

"It's easy. If you love him."

"Maybe for you. I was ready to leave the Ugly Stick and Temptation to move to Austin before I met Connor. Now I'm not sure. I'm afraid I'll get restless again. I don't want to marry Connor, then get bored and leave. I would hate myself forever if I hurt him."

"That tells me you love him."

"Yeah, but is love enough?"

"Oh, honey, it is if you're willing to put your man's needs above your own, and he's willing to do the same."

Charli shrugged. "Well, I'm not good at the commitment thing."

"You've been living with him going on almost a year. I'd say you're pretty well committed."

"Sort of, but marriage is so much more." Charli settled more bottles in the trough and straightened. "I'm not sure I'm ready."

"Can you imagine living without him?"

Charli's eyes widened. "Hell no."

"Then there you have it."

Charli smiled. "You make it sound easy."

Audrey shook her head. "Nothing's easy about relationships, whether you're married or living together. It helps when you're muddling through it all if you love each other. And I've seen you two together. There's love in spades."

"Thanks, Audrey. Once again, you're all full of advice for everyone else. You need to take some for yourself." Charli hugged her. "Relax. It will happen when it happens."

"Gah!" Audrey threw her hands in the air. "If I hear one more person say that, I'm liable to throw something. We've been married long enough I think it'll stick. But I'm in my thirties and not getting any younger."

"Please don't say you're getting old. You look like you're nineteen."

"But I'm not nineteen, Charli. I can hear my biological clock ticking so loudly I can't hear myself think. At one time in my life I thought owning my own business and having friends would be enough."

"You've accomplished more than most people have in their fifties."

"Sure. I have the Ugly Stick Saloon." She'd been so happy when she'd bought the bar, using her hard-earned stripping money. "I have the best employees I can trust and count as my friends."

"Darn right you do. And we'd do anything for you. You've bailed more than one of us out of tight spots."

"I thought this place was all I needed." Audrey stared

out across the saloon, packed with patrons. Friday night was always crowded. Her gaze gravitated toward the man she loved. "Until I met Jackson, I thought I had it all. Now I want more."

"And by more, you mean a family to call your own?"

Audrey nodded. "My life won't be complete until I have Jackson's children."

"You have our prayers and wishes. And you can count on me to babysit." Charli frowned. "Damn. You're making me rethink my position on marriage. All of the sudden, I've been bitten by the baby bug."

Audrey's heart lightened and she grabbed Charli's hands. "Wouldn't it be great if we were both pregnant at the same time? Our kids could grow up together."

"Whoa! Wait a minute. One step at a time." Charli pulled her hands free. "I promised my momma I'd wait to have children until I was properly married. I don't plan on breaking my promise to my mother, God rest her soul. Let's work on you first. You can pave the way and show me how easy it is before I commit to marriage, babies and the whole nine yards."

Audrey nodded. "Okay then. Let's see if my trucks are loaded with asphalt."

Charli's brows furrowed. "Huh?"

"I'm a few days late for my period. I hope to be paving soon." She squared her shoulders and reached beneath the bar for her purse and the pregnancy kit she'd tucked inside a week ago. Either way, she wanted to know whether or not she was pregnant.

"Oh, Audrey, that's great. I have my fingers crossed for you and Jackson." Charli held up both hands, displaying four sets of crossed fingers. "I'd cross my toes if I wasn't wearing these darned boots." She gave Audrey a nudge. "Go, pee on the stick or whatever it is you do with one of those. Do you want me to go with you?"

"No. I can manage on my own. I've been peeing by myself for thirty-two years." With excitement building, Audrey tried to catch Jackson's eye as she walked toward the hallway where the bathrooms were. He was deep in conversation with Mark and Luke. Probably about ranch business.

Oh well. She'd come out in a few minutes with their happy news. She had to believe the sixth time was a charm. It was going to happen.

Audrey entered the bathroom and tore open the box, her hands suddenly shaking, all her hopes for the future wrapped up in that one little box and the magic stick inside.

All she needed was to pee on the test strip, plug it into the stick and wait for the results. She'd even sprung for the more expensive test kit—the one that spelled it out. Either it would say *Pregnant* or *Not Pregnant*. No interpretation required.

When she hovered over the toilet, her knees shook and she struggled to let loose a stream of urine. The last couple of times, she'd had trouble with this, as if not peeing on the strip would change the results.

Drawing on Jackson and Charli's advice, she relaxed and eventually peed. Shoving the test stick beneath the warm urine, she almost dropped it, she was trembling so badly. Five seconds was all she needed. Thankfully, when she pulled it out, it was damp at the right end of the device.

As she waited the required three minutes, her breath lodged in her throat. Audrey checked her watch. One minute down, nothing on the display screen. She closed her eyes and counted to one hundred, opened her eyes and checked her watch. Two minutes down. A quick glance at the stick's display window and it was empty.

She took a ragged breath, her heart thundering, her eyes burning. Sitting on the toilet for the last minute was sheer torture. Closing her eyes, she prayed harder than she'd ever prayed before. *Please, God, give me a baby.*

Avoiding the test stick, she checked her watch. Four minutes had passed. Turning her gaze to the window, the first word she saw was *Pregnant.*

Her heart leaped into her throat before she saw the other word beside it.

As quickly as her hopes had skyrocketed, they crashed to the earth.

There in the display window were the two words she'd dreaded.

Not Pregnant.

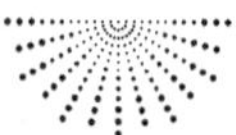

"How are things coming along with your family plan?" Luke asked when the conversation about the ranch had petered out.

Jackson glanced at the hallway that led toward the bathrooms. He'd seen Audrey duck back there, carrying her purse with what he suspected was the pregnancy test kit she'd told him about. As soon as he realized what she was about to do, he'd disconnected from the conversation with his brothers, his total focus on Audrey and the outcome of the test.

"Hey, Jackson." Mark waved a hand in front of Jackson's face. "Luke asked you a question."

Jackson dragged his gaze away from the hallway and glanced toward his brother Luke without really seeing him. "What was the question?" Immediately, his gaze returned to the hallway. What the hell was taking her so long?

"I asked if you liked purple people eaters," Luke said.

"Yeah, sure. Whatever. Order one for me." Jackson leaned forward, preparing to stand, when Mark busted out laughing.

"You should see yourself, bro." Mark slapped his thigh, his eyes brimming with tears of mirth. "You haven't heard one word we've said in the past five minutes."

"Sorry. Audrey went to the bathroom."

Mark grinned. "I'm all into Libby, but I don't follow her to the bathroom unless it's to share a shower, in which case, I'm there."

Luke backhanded his brother in the chest. "Back off, Mark. Jackson's obviously worried about Audrey."

His grin slipping from his face, Mark touched his brother's arm. "What's wrong? Is she sick?"

"Better yet… Is she pregnant?" Luke asked.

"I don't know." Jackson continued to stare at the hallway, willing Audrey to emerge. "I think she went in with an early pregnancy test kit."

Mark joined Jackson in his staring vigil. "How long has she been in there?"

Jackson glanced at his watch. "Over ten minutes."

"I didn't think those things took that long," Luke said.

"Since when did you become an expert on pregnancy tests?" Mark quipped.

Luke shrugged. "I read."

Jackson pushed to his feet. "I'm going to check on her."

About the time he rose, the music changed and the

waitresses pushed through the crowd to climb up on the bar.

The men in the saloon rose to their feet, clapping and shouting as the waitresses on the bar danced in unison to "Sin Wagon", an oldie by the Dixie Chicks.

With all the patrons of the bar on their feet, it made it difficult for Jackson to get from the barroom to the hallway with the bathrooms. When he finally reached the hallway, a man and woman were there, in a full-on, leg-sliding, hands-groping kiss, blocking the women's restroom.

"Excuse me," Jackson said.

The man and woman grunted but didn't stop their tonsil gymnastics.

Not caring if he started a fight, Jackson pushed past the two and barged into the women's restroom.

A woman in a crop top and short, flouncy skirt and cowboy boots looked up from the mirror. "Hey, cowboy, are you lost? Or are you looking for me?"

"I'm looking for Audrey. Have you seen her?"

"Strawberry-blonde, about so high?" The woman in the skirt raised her hand to about Audrey's height.

"Yes, ma'am."

"She ran out of here in tears a couple minutes ago." The woman's welcoming smile disappeared, a frown denting her brow. "Were you the one who made her cry?"

"No. Yes. Hell, I don't know." He spun on his heel and slammed back through the door, more anxious than ever to find Audrey. If she was crying, the news wasn't good. He pushed aside his own disappointment and went in search of her, praying she didn't do something stupid in her grief. Why couldn't she understand that she meant everything to him? They didn't need to have children to make their lives complete.

By the time he reached the hallway leading to the storeroom, backstage and rear exit, it had been closer to fifteen minutes since he'd seen Audrey head to the bathroom with the kit in hand. He hated to think of how torn up she would be about the negative test result. He was a man who liked to fix things. Give him a fence, he could restring barbwire like a pro. Broken corral panel? He'd have it measured, cut and nailed in no time. But this was one thing he couldn't fix, and it frustrated the hell out of him. Why did getting pregnant have to be so darned hard?

Jackson ducked into the storeroom where he and Audrey had made love earlier. No sign of his pretty wife. A quick run through the backstage area where she kept the costumes for the stripper shows turned up nothing. Jackson headed for the rear exit. If she was that badly upset, she might get in her truck and leave. He could only hope she headed home. But what if she didn't and she got in a wreck and he couldn't find her until...

His mind conjuring every bad scenario he could imagine, Jackson blew through the back exit and screeched to a halt so fast he almost fell on his face.

There in the far corner of the rear parking lot stood a beat-up old camper, towed by an equally derelict truck. The woman standing beside it was a small, dark-haired pixie with a heart-shaped face sporting dark shadows beneath her eyes.

Beside her stood Audrey, her face tear streaked, but a shaky smile pasted over her own sadness. She wrapped her arm around the smaller woman and hugged her.

Over the din of music radiating from inside the building, Jackson heard Audrey say, "You can work for me until you get on your feet."

He almost laughed out loud with the relief he felt. All Audrey needed was someone else to worry about to push her own disappointment aside.

This dark-haired waif in distress was just what Audrey needed.

Jackson sent a silent prayer of thanks to the gods of his Kiowa ancestors and stepped up to the two women. "Audrey, are you going to introduce me to your friend?"

Audrey lifted her ravaged face up to Jackson and brushed away a ready tear that slipped from the corner of her eye.

He squeezed her arm in recognition of her pain, smiled at the stranger and stuck out his hand. "I'm Jackson Gray Wolf. Audrey's husband."

The small woman laid her hand in his. It felt so tiny and fragile until she squeezed his hand with a firm grip. "I'm E—" She paused, pressed her lips together, then started over. "I'm Beth Smith." She turned toward Audrey, a worried frown wrinkling her pale skin, her hair hanging over her temple, almost blocking one of her eyes. "I was just telling your wife that I've run out of gas."

"We can help you get to a gas station." Jackson draped an arm over Audrey's shoulder.

She leaned against him, slipping her arm around his waist. "The truck stop at the highway junction in Temptation stays open twenty-four hours."

"I keep a spare gas can in the back of my truck," Jackson offered.

"I don't want to be any trouble. But I was also telling Audrey that not only did I run out of gas, I'm short on funds." She dipped her head.

Audrey smiled at the woman. "I offered to let her park her camper out back here until she earns enough money to fund her travels. She can work at the Ugly Stick Saloon."

Beth glanced at the saloon and back at the trailer. The hair over her temple shifted, exposing a purple bruise. "I'd love to help, but I'm not sure that I can."

Audrey shrugged. "Of course, you might not want to work in a saloon. I sometimes forget not everyone approves of drinking and dancing. No worries. I'm sure we can find something more suitable in Temptation."

Beth reached out for Audrey's hand. "No, it's not that I disapprove, it's just that I have...commitments—"

A small cry sounded from inside the camp trailer.

Audrey stiffened beside Jackson, the hand around his waist tightened and her fingernails dug into his skin.

"Excuse me. I was in the middle of feeding time." Beth spun and darted into the trailer as the cries became more urgent.

With each tiny cry Jackson's gut knotted more and

he sucked in a breath, preparing to catch Audrey as she fell apart.

The baby's cry reached into Audrey's heart and tugged hard. She tried to swallow past the lump in her throat. What cruel trick was God playing on her? She'd asked Him to give her a baby. Not flaunt another woman's baby at her as she continued to be barren, childless and empty.

Like a rubbernecker drawn to an auto accident, Audrey couldn't turn away, couldn't leave when her feet were firmly rooted to the ground. Her heart slowed to a dull, heavy plod as she waited for Beth to emerge from the trailer, a tiny infant in her arms.

Beth held the child and her face softened in a warm smile as she balanced the baby on her arm while holding a bottle with her other hand. Glancing up, she said, "This is Mia. My daughter."

Audrey couldn't make her mouth form words. She stood in dumb silence, her gaze riveted on the infant child.

Thankfully, Jackson could speak and he did. "Well hello, Mia." He leaned over the baby and touched her cheek. "How old is she?"

"One month and six days," Beth said, her voice little more than a whisper.

"Isn't it kind of soon to be on the road with one that small?" Jackson noted.

Beth glanced away, her lips thinning. "We had no choice. I'd reached the end of my…lease. I had to leave."

"Where are you headed? Maybe we can help you get there," Jackson offered.

Audrey stood stock-still, a solid lump lodged firmly in her throat, taking it all in but unable to offer any words of advice or comfort when her own heart was breaking.

She wasn't pregnant. Holding her own baby in her arms was never further out of her reach than at that moment.

Again Beth stared off into the distance, anywhere but at Jackson. "I'm headed west."

"Is your family expecting you? You could always use the phone inside if you'd like to call. Cell phones are not very reliable out here." Jackson waved a hand toward the saloon.

"No." Beth's eyes widened. "No, I don't have any family. It's just me and Mia."

"I could pull the trailer to a campground tomorrow. You might be more comfortable with hookups than back here behind the saloon."

"If you don't mind, I'd like to stay here for at least the night. I've been on the road for twelve hours. It's hard on Mia and we're both just so very tired."

Audrey's empathy finally pushed past the heartache of seeing baby Mia. "There's no question about it. You can stay here as long as you need to. And we can help you out with money for gas, food or whatever you need until you're on your feet."

Beth pushed her shoulders back and lifted her chin. "I won't take charity. I can work as long as I can find a babysitter to care for Mia while I do."

"Of course. I'm sure we can help you out with that as well. Between me and Jackson, we know a lot of folks in the community. I'm sure someone would be happy to keep an eye on Mia."

The frown furrowing Beth's brow lifted, and she gave Audrey a tired smile. "Thank you. You don't know how much this means to me."

"Are you sure you don't have anyone you need to contact to let them know where you are and that you're okay?" Audrey asked.

Beth shook her head. "I don't have any family. None."

"Okay." Audrey lifted her hands in surrender. "I just can't imagine traveling such a long way with an infant so young."

"We'll be fine, won't we, Mia?" Beth leaned down and kissed the baby's cheek.

"She's a beautiful baby." Jackson touched the baby's cheek again.

"Do you want to hold her?" Beth asked, holding the baby out to Audrey.

Audrey's chest squeezed so hard she could barely breathe. "No, thank you."

"I do." Jackson held out his hands.

Beth laid the infant in his arms, glancing up at him nervously.

"I promise not to drop her." Jackson smiled reassuringly.

She handed him the bottle. "If you brush it across her lips, she'll latch on."

Following her instruction, Jackson slid the milky nipple across the infant's lips.

Like a baby bird, Mia opened her mouth and followed the nipple until Jackson slipped it in. With a sigh, she sucked on the bottle, her eyes closed, her tiny fist pressed against her cheek.

Jackson looked so natural. The towering Native American with his swarthy skin and big hands held the baby like she was made of glass, cradled in his arm, letting her suckle from the bottle. Jackson would be a great father.

Audrey ached inside and would have turned and walked away if Beth hadn't stepped up to her and hugged her neck. "Thank you for helping me. I was beginning to lose hope."

With a great amount of effort, Audrey pushed aside her own disappointment and hugged the woman back. "You'll be okay. You're among friends here. We'll help you get on your feet."

"God bless you," Beth whispered.

"Do you have a shower and bathroom facilities in your trailer?" Jackson asked.

"I do. I have enough water for another day or two. Then I'll have to get to a campsite for the hookups. I really didn't think ahead when I left yesterday morning, or I would have filled the tanks and pantry."

"Do you have enough formula and diapers for Mia?"

She smiled. "I have enough for the week. After that..." Beth's lips twisted. "I suppose the sooner I start earning money, the better."

"Don't you worry about a thing." Audrey clapped her hands, determined to pull herself together and think about someone other than herself. "I know at least half a dozen women who'd give their eyeteeth to hold sweet Mia through the evening hours while you're working. And that will leave you all day to spend with your daughter."

"That would be a wonderful if you can refer someone to me. I've never left Mia with anyone and I don't know a soul around here."

Audrey nodded. "I'd be glad to. For the most part, people are friendly and eager to help."

"If you and Jackson are any indication, I'd believe it." Beth held out her arms for Mia.

Jackson handed her over, easing the baby into her mother's hold. "She's so small."

"She was three weeks premature. But she's up to seven pounds already."

"I've held puppies bigger than Mia." Jackson shook his head. "Are you sure she's old enough to travel?"

"If I'd had any other choice, I wouldn't have moved her." She held the baby up to her shoulder and patted her back until the baby released an air bubble in a whisper of a burp.

A cool Texas wind feathered across Audrey's skin. "Are you sure you two will be warm enough in that trailer? The temperature is supposed to drop down into the low fifties."

"If I could plug into an outlet, I can run the blower. I have propane for heat."

"You feel safe with it?" Audrey asked.

"I've camped in the trailer before. We'll be okay."

Beth cradled Mia on one arm and touched Audrey's arm with one hand. "Really, I don't mean to be a bother."

"Dear Lord, Beth, you're not a bother. I'm worried about the baby. She's so small."

Beth smiled down at Mia. "We'll be fine. Won't we, sweetheart?" she repeated as if reassuring herself as much as the baby.

"Do you at least have a carbon monoxide detector in the trailer?" Audrey persisted.

Beth glanced up. "No, I don't."

Audrey shot a look toward Jackson. "What happened to the one I bought for the saloon?"

"It's probably still in the package in the storeroom where I left it." Jackson held up a hand. "I'll get it and install it right now."

"Oh please, you don't have to," Beth said.

"It would be my pleasure." Jackson ducked back into the saloon, leaving Audrey with Beth and Mia.

Audrey stood awkwardly. "Perhaps you should take Mia back inside. I wouldn't want her to catch a cold."

"It is getting chilly. Won't you come in?" Beth led the way. "It's not much, but it's my home for the time being."

Audrey followed, curious about Beth and Mia's living arrangements. She told herself it was because they'd be parked at the back of the saloon and, since it was on Ugly Stick property, as a business owner, she was liable for her. The truth was she wanted to make sure Beth had adequate accommodations for the tiny infant.

The small trailer had a stovetop, a single bed at the

back and a bathroom so little a man as broad-shouldered as Jackson wouldn't be able to turn around inside. The recreational vehicle had to be at least thirty years old. Corners and edges were worn smooth and the enamel was chipped in the sink and on the stove. But it was clean and Beth had enough blankets to keep herself and Mia warm. A portable bassinet lay on the floor beside the bed, with a soft crocheted pink blanket folded neatly inside.

Everything about Mia made Audrey's breath catch.

"Could you hold her for a moment while I move things around?" Beth shoved the baby into Audrey's arms. "Since she just ate, she'll probably sleep for the next couple of hours."

Audrey took the baby because she had no other option. Holding Mia, she was amazed at how light and warm she was. The baby's cupid-bow mouth moved as if she still sucked on the bottle. Her pink cheeks looked so soft Audrey had to touch one.

She brushed Mia's cheek with her fingertip, and it was every bit as velvety smooth as it looked. The sweet scent of baby powder wafted around her, and she felt her knees weaken and her nipples tighten in an instinctive maternal response. Intense longing struck her so hard she could barely breathe.

So this was what it felt like to be a mother.

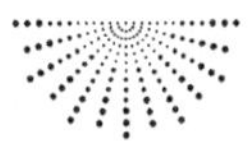

CHAPTER THREE

Jackson stretched out on the king-size bed in the house he'd been raised in and in which he hoped to raise his own children soon. He remembered being a little boy, climbing up in the bed with his mother and father. Back before the twins were born. He'd had his folks all to himself and felt loved and special. When Mark and Luke were born there were just more people in the big bed and no less love.

He'd told Audrey he would be just fine if it was just the two of them, but he hoped for a little girl with strawberry-blond hair or a boy or two who looked like Mark and Luke when they'd been little. Dark hair, dark eyes and full of mischief.

After they'd left the Ugly Stick, he knew he had to do something to cheer his wife. The effort they'd gone through over the past six months was wearing on her spirit, and that was not like Audrey. She was the toughest, most resilient woman he knew. He'd come up with a plan, and while she had been at the saloon peeing on a stick in the bathroom, he'd made a few calls and had tomorrow all set up.

Audrey emerged from the bathroom, wearing a short, baby-doll nightgown that showed off her long, slender legs. He remembered the night she'd danced for him on his birthday. The night he'd known for certain that she was the woman for him. She'd worn a tiny vest, chaps and those bright red cowboy boots. Even though she'd been wearing a wig and mask, he'd known it was her.

Now she paced the length of the room and back, the filmy, blue nightgown swirling around her hips with every turn, her rose-tipped nipples peeking through the sheer fabric.

The more she paced, the hotter she looked and the harder Jackson's cock grew.

Ten laps and she still hadn't spoken a word.

Jackson couldn't stand it a moment longer. "Hey." He patted the mattress beside him. "Sit before you wear a hole in the flooring."

She glanced up at him as if seeing him for the first time. "Oh sorry. I was just thinking."

He chuckled. "That part I got. Do you want to tell me about the pregnancy test?"

Her eyes filled and she shook her head.

"Okay." He wasn't really good at the game of twenty questions, but if that was what it took to draw Audrey out, he'd do it. The woman was obviously distraught. "Are you disappointed about the results?"

"Yes, but I don't want to talk about it."

"If you don't want to talk about it, what *do* you want to talk about?"

Audrey bit her bottom lip and sighed. "Beth and Mia."

Jackson was afraid of that. "What about them?"

"I'm worried about them staying in that old trailer. It's supposed to be cold tonight."

"They'll be just fine."

"What if they run out of propane?"

"I checked the tank and it's three-quarters full. They won't run out in one night."

"What if the carbon monoxide detector doesn't work?"

"We tested it after I installed it." His lips twitched at the memory of how high Audrey had jumped at the beeping noise it emitted. "The device will work." He patted the bed again. "Sit. You've been on your feet over ten hours."

"I'm fine."

"Worrying about Beth and Mia isn't going to accomplish anything. Sleep and you can come up with a new plan for the two of them tomorrow."

Audrey chewed on that damned lower lip again, making Jackson crazy. He wanted to pull that lip into his mouth and suck on it, then kiss her silly.

"You really think they'll be okay?" she asked, twisting the hem of her nightgown, exposing her flat belly and the lacy thong underwear she wore just for him.

Jackson nearly came out of the bed with his need to grab Audrey and lick a path from her cute little belly-button all the way down to… "They will be just fine," he said through gritted teeth.

Audrey glanced toward the door as if debating whether or not to go check for herself. "They're so far away. If Beth needs help, she won't have any way to contact us or the sheriff. I should have left her a key to the saloon so that she could use the phone in case of an emergency."

"You can do that tomorrow. What you need now is sleep. And by the look of Beth, she could use some too. Disturbing her at one o'clock in the morning won't help her."

Audrey's shoulders slumped. "I know. I should have offered to let her stay here." She climbed into the bed and lay on top of the comforter. "At least here she'd have backup. No woman should have to raise a baby on her own. It's hard enough with both parents. A lone woman, raising an infant baby, has to be tough."

Audrey rolled toward the side of the bed.

If Jackson didn't stop her, she'd return to the Ugly Stick Saloon, collect Beth and Mia and bring them back to the Gray Wolf Ranch. She swung her legs over the side of the big bed.

Before she could put her feet on the floor, Jackson snagged her around the middle and yanked her onto the bed, flat on her back.

He pinned her delicate yet capable wrists high above her head and stared down at her. "Did anyone ever tell you that you're beautiful when you worry?"

A tiny dent formed in the middle of her forehead.

He kissed the dent. "Well, you are. Especially when

you frown so fiercely. Some women would only look bitchy. You're positively hot."

Audrey shook her head, the hint of a smile quirking her lips. "Jackson, you're so full of it."

"No, you are—"

Her frown returned.

He smoothed the frown away with another kiss. "You're full of love for everyone else. It's one of the reasons I love you so much."

Audrey's eyes filled. "I wasn't ready for it."

"For what?"

"Holding the baby," Audrey whispered.

"Oh, honey. If it makes you feel better, I can help her move the trailer to an RV park tomorrow."

"No. They shouldn't be penalized because I'm a big whiny mess."

"Penalized? An RV park might be quieter and have the amenities Beth will need to provide a home for Mia."

Audrey chewed on her lip. "I don't want them to move unless Beth wants to move. I like her. And Mia..." A tear slipped down her cheek. "She's beautiful. And so tiny. Holding her was one of the most rewarding and frightening things I've done in my entire life."

"Just wait until you're holding your own."

"Oh, Jackson. I'm not pregnant and I started my period tonight." More tears trickled down her cheek. "We can't even make love."

"It's okay, sweetheart. Maybe next time."

She shook her head. "I can't do this anymore. It's killing me."

"Okay, then. We won't try." Jackson's chest tightened at the sadness in Audrey's voice. She'd always been the optimist. She'd never met a challenge she couldn't undertake. For her to give up was unheard of. But that was what she was doing.

Jackson swallowed hard on the lump forming in his throat. He wanted children. With Audrey. But he wanted Audrey to be happy, no matter what decision she made. She was the only woman for him. If it was to be just the two of them together forever, that'd have to be good enough for him. "It'll be all right. Don't be sad. Just relax and stop thinking about it. We can go back to the way we were before we decided to have children. Sound good?"

Audrey's bottom lip trembled as she nodded her head. "Are you sure you're okay with that? I mean, just the two of us?"

"Yes, oh yes. Just promise me you'll start smiling again. I miss the happy Audrey who always looks on the bright side of everything."

"It's been hard lately."

"I know. You put too much pressure on yourself. Just forget about having babies and enjoy everything else life has to offer. You have me. Luke, Mark and Libby, and the entire crew at the Ugly Stick would lay down their lives for you. Babe, you are so very much loved."

Audrey sniffed and swiped at the trail of tears on her cheek. "I love my family and wouldn't trade it for the world."

"Even me?" He winked. "Even when I snore?"

"Even you." She smiled and cupped Jackson's face. "I

love you, Jackson Gray Wolf." Then she kissed him and pressed her body close to his. "What would I do without you?"

"Now that's something you really should never think about. I plan on being around a long, long time. So get used to that idea." He smoothed her hair back from her face and drew her into his arms, his hand skimming down her back and up under her nightgown, splaying across her naked back. He couldn't touch her enough to be completely satisfied. She was his addiction, the one thing he could never live without.

"So tomorrow is a whole new day. I declare it Audrey Anderson Day. Pamper yourself. Have your hair done. Get a mani-pedi or whatever it is you ladies do to your nails. Paint them every color of the rainbow if it makes you smile."

"Do you hear yourself?" Audrey laughed. "I'll be fine."

"Good. And don't think about anything but being happy."

"Okay." Audrey lay back against the pillow, a smile already curling her pretty lips.

"Promise?" Jackson kissed the tip of her nose and each cheek.

"I promise." Audrey caught his face between her palms. "For you."

"Good. I've already talked with Mona. She has a spot for you on her schedule to do your hair and nails."

Audrey's eyes narrowed. "When did you have time to plan all this?"

"While you were working at the bar." Jackson

grinned. "Actually, it was Charli and Kendall's idea. While you were in the bathroom, I made the call to Mona. I think I interrupted her and Grant in the middle of something. There was a lot of giggling and squeals on Mona's part."

"You're terrible. What time did you call them?"

"Must have been around midnight."

"They have day jobs."

"Hey, they weren't sleeping."

"Still…"

"It was an emergency and Mona agreed. She scheduled you over her lunch hour."

"I can't have Mona give up her lunch."

"I'll have it catered in." Jackson's brows rose in challenge. "Any more excuses?"

Audrey shook her head. "No."

"Good. Charli and Kendall are going along as moral support and will take you shopping for something naughty afterward."

Audrey's lips twisted as if she fought a smile. "For you or for me?"

"You, of course. If it's really sexy, I promise not to be too aroused."

"The hell you won't be." She palmed his chest. "And you damn well better be aroused if I go to all the trouble of shopping for it."

"Baby, you know it doesn't take much to get me all hot and bothered. You can wear absolutely nothing and I'll be in a lather before you can say *ready*." To prove it, Jackson shoved the pale blue nightie over her head and tossed it across the iron headboard. "See? I'm as stiff as a red-hot poker." He nudged her thigh with the evidence.

"Damn it, and I'm on my period." She touched his erection through the fabric of his boxers. "What a shame to waste it."

"I can wait."

"Maybe I can't." She slipped out of the grip he had on her wrists and wiggled her way down the bed until her face was in line with his shorts. Slipping her fingers in the elastic band, she shoved them down over his hips until his dick sprang free, thick, hard and straining to get at her.

"We could make love in the shower," Jackson suggested.

"I have a better idea." She grasped his member in her warm hands and slid them upward to the tip and back down to the base. She rolled his balls in the fingers of one hand while guiding him to her lips. "Yeah, I think I have an excellent idea." She pulled one of his knees over her until he straddled her head. "Now, let's see what you can do with this big, bad boy." She took him into her mouth, licking at the tip of his cock.

Jackson fought to hold back and let her take the lead. When her hands closed over his buttocks, he was a goner. He thrust into her mouth and she took all of him until he bumped against the back of her throat. She pushed him out, scraping his length lightly with her teeth.

She was so warm and wet he thrust into her again, and her fingers tightened on his ass, holding him deep inside her, while her tongue slipped around him, lapping and twirling along his length.

His groin tightened so much he didn't think he would last two seconds. When she guided him into a faster rhythm, he was more than willing to comply, pumping in and out of her mouth until the tension built to a fevered pitch. He started to pull out of her, knowing if he waited too long, he'd shoot his wad into her mouth.

She refused to let go of him, holding on to his cock as long as he could stand.

He resisted, his control stretched so very thin.

Finally she released him.

Jackson pulled free and ejaculated across her chest and neck.

Audrey held his cock, a smile curving her lips. "I told you I have good ideas."

"The very best." He left the bed and entered the bathroom, returning with a warm, wet washcloth. As he cleaned her chest and neck, he bent to capture those rosy lips with his. She tasted of him. "I could never get tired of making love with you."

"Mmm. Same goes for me." She blinked sleepily. "I'll be glad when my monthly is over."

"Me too." Jackson returned the cloth to the bathroom and climbed into bed, spooning the sleepy Audrey against his body, wishing he could make everything all right for her. She did so much for everyone else; just once, everything should work out for her. Jackson fell to sleep dreaming of holding Audrey's baby in his arms. Audrey stood beside him, her face flushed with happiness. It all felt so real, he didn't want to wake up.

"So what's it to be? Carmel highlights, streaks of peacock blue, hot pink, neon orange?" Mona asked as she secured a cape around Audrey's neck and combed out her long, wet hair. "The sky's the limit. Jackson's buying."

Audrey laughed at her friend and beautician. "Just trim it a little and give me a younger hairstyle. I have to look great to shop with Charli and Kendall. They're so much younger than me."

Charli snorted. "Oh go on. You are absolutely ageless."

Kendall nodded. "So true. I hope to look as good as you do when I'm forty."

Audrey's brows drew together and she lifted a sponge roller from Mona's tray of hairstyling tools. "I'm not forty!" She lobbed the roller at Kendall. It missed and bounced off Charli's head.

"Hey. I think you don't look a day over twenty-five. Kendall's the one who's the baby among us." As soon as Charli said the word *baby*, Kendall backhanded her.

Charli's eyes widened and she clapped a hand over her mouth. "Sorry."

"Why?" Audrey stared from Kendall to Charli and back. "What's going on here?"

Kendall sighed. "Jackson made us promise not to mention the B-word today."

A mix of love and anger washed over Audrey. "Good

grief. I'm not fragile. I'm not going to break or anything. Saying the word *baby* isn't going to send me off the deep end."

"Well, we did promise," Mona admitted.

"As Jackson declared this Audrey Anderson Day, I'm the queen and I officially release you from the promise. There will be no walking on eggshells today or any day."

Charli sagged. "Whew! I was wondering how I'd keep my big mouth shut all day."

"Yeah, especially since you hired Beth," Kendall said. "What's the scoop?"

Audrey shook her head. "All I know is that she had to leave her apartment and only has the trailer to live in. Poor girl had been on the road for twelve hours."

"Where's she headed?"

Audrey hadn't really been able to think much past baby Mia. "I'm not sure. She said she didn't have any family."

Mona dragged a comb through her hair, working the tangles free a little at a time. "That makes no sense to be on the road for twelve hours and not be headed anywhere in particular. And what made her take the back roads that led her to the Ugly Stick Saloon?"

Audrey shrugged. "I really don't know."

A long, pregnant pause followed.

Charli shook her head, staring from Kendall to Mona. "You two aren't going to mention the elephant in the room? That's right, leave it to me, the big mouth." She turned her gaze on Audrey. "The woman has an infant that can't be more than two weeks old."

"Mia's a month old. She was a preemie," Audrey corrected.

"My point is," Charli continued, "women don't go on twelve-hour road trips with newborns, headed nowhere. Something's not right. You should have Deputy Cramer run a background check on her. Maybe she's wanted for a crime."

Kendall's eyes widened. "Maybe she stole the baby."

Audrey shook her head. "The baby looks like her."

"Babies look like babies," Charli disagreed. "The woman could be lying to you and on the run. What would it hurt to run the check on her license? Tell her you have to make a copy of it for employment at the Ugly Stick."

"I suppose I could do that." Audrey didn't like being dishonest or subversive. She took most people at face value. "Beth looks like the real deal. I trust her."

"Then let *me* have the deputy run the check." Charli dug in her purse and pulled out a crinkled napkin with writing on it. "Look, I wrote down her license plate number. I can have Cramer run it if you're not comfortable asking for her driver's license."

"Okay, I'll think about it. Either way, don't be obvious about your suspicions when you're around her. She appears to have been through a lot, having been uprooted and starting over with a tiny infant."

"If the infant is *hers*," Kendall repeated. "Think about the mother she could have stolen it from."

Mona clipped a portion of Audrey's hair up on top of her head and reached for the blow-dryer. "I'd have

Cramer check the missing persons reports and see if anyone had a baby stolen."

"Good grief. Beth's on the up and up." Audrey waved her hand like a queen, tipping her head back. "Now, can we drop the topic and get on with my day? It is, after all, Audrey Anderson Day."

"Absolutely, your highness." Kendall genuflected in a low curtsy and giggled, destroying the effect.

An hour later, her fingernails shining a lovely shade of rose-petal pink, Audrey, Charli and Kendall hugged Mona and set off on their mission to visit the newest shop in Temptation, temptingly named Naughty Nothings.

As they passed the hardware store and the sheriff's office, Charli stopped. "I just remembered that Connor wanted me to check and see if his new drill gun has arrived at the hardware store. It will only take a moment. I'll meet you at the shop."

Audrey's gaze zeroed in on Charli. "If you're thinking about stopping at the sheriff's office, don't."

Charli's cheeks flushed red and she raised her hands in surrender. "No, really, Connor has a drill gun on order. One of those cordless types. He's been waiting for over a week. It should be in by now."

The telltale blush in Charli's cheeks was enough for Audrey to know she was fibbing. What would it hurt to have Deputy Cramer check on Beth's background? She was certain he'd find nothing, but her friends wouldn't rest until they knew for sure Beth wasn't out to take advantage of Audrey.

Audrey smiled. She had really great friends, a

wonderful husband and brothers-in-law. What more could she ask for?

A baby.

An image of Jackson holding the tiny Mia in his arms ripped through her mind, making her heart ache. She pushed the image aside and glanced from Kendall to Charli. "Go on. Check on the drill. And while you're at it, have Cramer run Beth's license plate."

CHAPTER FOUR

Jackson sat at the bar inside the Ugly Stick Saloon that evening, nursing a beer and looking for every opportunity he could muster to corner Audrey in the storeroom and make her tell him what she'd purchased at the Naughty Nothings store on Main Street. Every time Charli or Kendall passed him with a tray loaded with drinks, they smiled knowingly.

He didn't always come to the bar at night. He had a ranch to run during the daylight hours, but the house was too lonely without Audrey. Since Mark and Luke had built their own home to share with Libby, the ranch house they'd grown up in was too big and too quiet for Jackson all by himself. Audrey had been swapping out late nights with Charli, but Friday and Saturday were usually all hands on deck. Cowboys came out of the fields for a cold beer, pretty girls and country music to tap their boots to.

Dusty Cramer, one of the county sheriff's deputies, slipped onto the stool beside Jackson. He wasn't in uniform and he ordered a beer. Wearing a regular cowboy hat, he was just another cowboy at the saloon to have a good time.

"Jackson." Cramer lifted his foaming mug.

"Dusty." Jackson tapped his to the edge of Cramer's. "Since you're off duty, here's to an uneventful night at the saloon."

He nodded. "Thanks." Then he tipped the mug back and took a long, deep pull on the beer before setting the mug on the bar and wiping his mouth with the back of his hand. "I hear you have a squatter on the premises."

Jackson sipped at his beer, knowing Dusty had more to say and would get around to it in his own sweet time. "We do." He tipped his head toward Beth as she weaved her way among the patrons of the bar, serving drinks with a sweet smile. "Her name's Beth Smith."

"Is that what she told you?"

Jackson shrugged. "Sure. Why?"

"Just wondered. I ran the plates on her truck and trailer. They expired over three years ago."

"So she's not so good at keeping up her licenses. I take it you also ran a background check on her."

Dusty stared into his beer. "Audrey can be too trusting of the strays she brings in."

With a nod, Jackson let Dusty continue.

"Charli and Kendall were worried. They wanted me to make sure the woman was on the up and up."

Jackson set his beer on the bar and faced Cramer. He hoped and prayed Beth wasn't wanted for murder or something. Having always trusted his gut, he couldn't believe the woman would harm a fly. "What did you find out?"

"Not much. The truck and trailer belonged to an older couple, Martha and Gordon Peterson."

"Belonged?"

"The couple is deceased as of four years ago."

"Damn." Jackson's gaze shifted from Beth to Audrey. What would Audrey think about her latest stray? "You don't think she stole the vehicles, do you?"

"I don't know what to think."

"And her name might not even be Beth Smith."

"That's about it." Deputy Cramer glanced across the room at the petite brunette who looked as harmful as a kitten. "I came to check her out for myself."

"Has the sheriff gotten wind of her? Does he know you've run her plates?"

"Not yet. Hopefully he won't find out anything until I've done a little more digging." Dusty's gaze followed Beth's every move. "I'd like to find out what I can without tipping her off. If she did steal the vehicles, I have to haul her in."

"Nice." Jackson stared at his beer mug now, wondering if all the baby talk and seeing Mia had biased him in Beth's favor. He couldn't imagine her in hand-cuffs. She seemed so nice. "So, what are you going to do?"

"I'm going to try and ask her some questions without alerting her to the fact I'm with the sheriff's department. Maybe she has the truck and trailer legally. If that's the case, all I could do is write tickets if I catch her out on the road driving with expired tags."

Jackson shook his head. "There has to be a story behind those sad eyes."

"What worries me most is the baby. What if she stole it? What if that baby is not hers? I'll try and lift some prints."

"She looks so innocent. Like she wouldn't harm a fly, and she's very good with the baby." Jackson glanced across at Beth.

Dusty's lips thinned. "Looks can be deceiving."

"Want me to disable her vehicle?"

"You might consider it. If she is on the run, she won't get too far with a baby and a broken-down truck. At the very least, it would keep me from giving her a ticket."

"Will do." Jackson slid off the bar stool, about to do his civic duty and pull the wiring on Beth's starter. All the years he'd been a straight shooter, always obeying the laws, setting the right example for his younger brothers, and here he was about to vandalize a young mother's vehicle.

Hell, if she was running away from something, she likely had a good reason. If Dusty didn't get to the bottom of it, Jackson sure as hell would. Mia needed a stable home, not a mother on the run from the law. Perhaps Beth was trying to get away from an abusive husband. Given the shadows under her eyes and the bruise on her temple and the fact she wasn't headed anywhere in particular, that scenario rang truer than anything.

In which case, Audrey would be the first to offer the

woman sanctuary. For that matter, so would Jackson. He had no patience for men who used their superior strength to bully women. And the thought of a man harming one hair on Mia's tiny head…well, it just wouldn't happen as long as Jackson had a breath left in him.

While Cramer sought out a seat in Beth's section of the saloon, Jackson went in search of his lovely wife. She needed to be aware of what Cramer had learned and prepare herself for the likelihood of Beth being hauled away in the back of a sheriff's cruiser. Hell, if Beth had kidnapped the baby, Audrey might be accused of harboring a criminal.

He found her in the storeroom, shifting boxes of whiskey and vodka around. Jackson took a heavy box from her arms. "Where?"

She pointed to a stack in one corner. "I could swear I ordered a case of Jack Daniels." She stood in the middle of the storeroom, wearing her cutoff shorts, a white blouse unbuttoned and tied around her middle, displaying a generous amount of midriff, and cleavage pushed up by a sequined corset that matched her studded red boots. It was just one of her uniforms for her work at the Ugly Stick Saloon. The patrons loved the women to dress sexy and provide an occasional dance or sing a song. That and tossing bottles like jugglers kept them entertained and coming back for more than the beer and whiskey.

Jackson set the box of whiskey on the stack she'd indicated and turned, taking her into his arms. "Hey beautiful."

She leaned into him and sighed. "Some nights I wonder why I own a bar. I could be home with my feet up, watching some mindless show on television. Instead, I'm searching through cases of booze, looking for the elusive box of Jack Daniels. What kind of life is that?"

Jackson grabbed her hands. "Sell this place, Audrey. Stay home with me and let me take care of you."

"Oh, Jackson. You know I couldn't let you do that. I love being an independent woman. I'm with you because I *want* to be, not because I *have* to be. I wouldn't have it any other way." She leaned up on her red-booted toes and kissed him on the lips. "Now, help me find that whiskey, will ya?"

He pulled her into his arms. "I will. After I get a proper kiss."

"Mine wasn't good enough?" She chuckled. "Suppose you show me how it's done, cowboy." She tipped her face up and closed her eyes. "I'm waiting."

He cupped her cheeks with both hands and bent to capture her lips with his. At first gentle, he brushed lightly across the softness of her mouth. That didn't last long before he was so hungry for her he couldn't hold back. He gathered her closer, lifted her by the backs of her thighs and backed her against the wall. His tongue dove between her teeth, thrusting and sliding along the length of hers, loving that she tasted sweet and tangy like strawberries with a hint of whipped cream.

When he finally set her on her feet, her eyes were glazed and her hands curled into the fabric of his shirt. "Okay, you win. That was a proper kiss." She pushed her hair back from her face, inhaled and let the air out in a long, slow stream. "Well, now, was that all you came in here for?"

Jackson had to think before he could remember why he'd sought out Audrey in the first place. "Deputy Cramer ran the tags on Beth's vehicles. Both the truck and the trailer tags expired over three years ago."

"So?" Audrey frowned. "She might not have had time to renew them before she had to leave."

"The original owners of the tags died four years ago."

Audrey blinked. "You think she killed them?"

"No, of course not. But there is a possibility she stole the vehicles."

"If she did, she had to have a really good, legitimate reason. From what I've observed of Beth so far, she's hardworking, cares about others and is dedicated to her baby. Every break she gets, she runs out to the trailer to check on Mia and Mona."

"You got Mona Daley to babysit? I'm surprised Grant let her out of his sight." Jackson pushed aside some of the boxes, searching for the case of Jack Daniels.

Audrey did the same, lifting a case of rum and moving it to another stack. "Grant is on the road right now, helping Sam Whitefeather compete at the National Finals Rodeo in Las Vegas. They left today and won't be back for at least a week. More if they decide to stay and enjoy some gambling in Sin City."

"I thought he gave up the rodeo?" Jackson went through a stack of five boxes without finding the whiskey. He reached up to shift some boxes on a shelf.

"Grant did, but he's going along to help Sam through the finals. Sam's riding broncs and roping with his new partner."

"Have you been out to check on Mona and Mia?"

Audrey frowned. "No. Why?"

"As worried as you were last night, I just wondered."

"After I introduced Beth to Mona, they took it from there. Beth seems quite happy to have Mona care for Mia."

"What about when Grant gets back?"

Audrey stood with her hands resting on her hips, staring around the storeroom. "I'll help Beth find another caregiver for Mia. Maybe by then she'll know what she wants to do."

"You mean she'll have enough money to move on."

Audrey reached for a case sitting on a shelf at eye level and turned it around. "I suppose." She snorted, straightened the box and then faced Jackson. "Damn. No whiskey. Honestly, Jackson, I don't see how she can keep moving with the baby. That poor child needs a stable environment."

"I'm surprised you haven't offered to put up Beth and Mia at the ranch yet."

Audrey chewed on her bottom lip. "As a matter of fact, I've been meaning to ask you—"

Jackson raised his hand. "You know my answer. Do what makes you happy, sweetheart." Once again he gathered her in his arms. "I just ask that you wait until we're more certain of her. If by some weird chance she has committed a crime, I don't want you to go to jail for her."

Audrey touched a finger to his chest. "Or you for that matter." She nodded. "I'll play it by ear. I take it Cramer is going to do more digging?"

"Yes, ma'am."

"I'll wait for him to come back with more details. But if the weather turns colder, I'm bringing them in."

"I agree."

"Good. Now help me find that case of whiskey or I'll have some cranky cowboys on my hands."

AUDREY KEPT a close watch on Beth through the weekend and into the next week. The weather held good, staying above the low fifties with sunshine and no rain.

For some reason Beth's truck wouldn't start. No matter how much Jackson fiddled with it, he couldn't seem to get it going. Audrey found that odd since Jackson was so good with anything mechanical. Beth refused to take it to Nick McBride's auto shop.

"I can't afford to pay anyone to fix the truck right now. Every penny I make needs to go into groceries and diapers for Mia," was Beth's response.

Audrey had to admit she was a little relieved the truck wouldn't run. Without a vehicle to tow the little camp trailer, Beth couldn't leave in the middle of the night. On the following Monday morning, Audrey stopped by and offered to take Beth shopping at the grocery store in Temptation.

Beth strapped Mia into an infant car seat and buckled it into the backseat of Audrey's truck. Then she climbed in. "Thank you for taking me to the store. I'm down to my last diaper and can of formula. It's amazing how many diapers Mia goes through in a week."

Audrey glanced back at the baby in the car seat.

Mia slept, perfectly content.

"Is she always this good traveling?" Audrey asked.

Beth laughed. "Until she gets tired of it. Twelve hours was too much. Even she needs to be able to stretch out occasionally."

Audrey pulled out of the parking lot behind the saloon. "Are you two doing okay in the trailer?"

"Oh yes. I really appreciate that you're letting me stay where I am."

"I can have Jackson hook up his truck to the trailer and take it to the local campground, where I'm certain you can find a slot for rent."

"That would be great, except I wouldn't be able to get back and forth to the saloon without my truck. And right now, I can't afford to have it fixed."

Audrey nodded. She had to bite back an offer for the two of them to stay at the ranch. She'd promised Jackson that she would wait a little longer, though her instinct to provide shelter for them was so strong it physically hurt not to say something. "At the very least, Jackson can take the trailer off to the campground to use their waste dump."

"That would be great. At least until I can afford to have the truck worked on."

"I can spot you the money to have it fixed," Audrey said. It wasn't inviting Beth into her home, but it would help the woman out, and she could have Nick take his time until they learned more about Beth.

"No. I wouldn't dream of it. I don't want to be indebted to anyone. Especially to you. You've already done so much for me."

"Me? My motives were purely selfish. I needed a good waitress and you fit the bill perfectly. You do good work."

Beth blushed. "Thank you. I admit I've never been a waitress."

"Well, you could have fooled me." Audrey focused on the road ahead. "What did you do in your former job?"

Out of the corner of her eye, Audrey could see Beth's face blanch, and she stared out the passenger window. "I've never actually had a job outside the home."

"No? How did you survive?"

"I married straight out of high school."

"Mia's father?" Audrey asked softly.

Beth shot a glance her way, her eyes wide. For a moment, she hesitated with her answer, then she replied softly, "Yes."

"I take it things didn't end well with him?"

"You could say that," she said noncommittally.

The inside of the truck became a silent tomb. Audrey had to screw up her nerve to ask the next question. "Beth, did he abuse you?"

"I'd rather not talk about it."

Audrey gave her a minute of reflection before she said, "I was in an abusive relationship before I moved to Temptation. I know what it feels like to hurt and how hard it is to step away from it all."

"Please." Beth swiped at the cheek turned away from Audrey as if wiping away a tear. "Can we change the subject?"

"Certainly." Audrey kept driving. "How's it working out with Mona watching Mia?"

Beth inhaled and let out a shaky breath. "Great. Mona is a natural with babies."

Audrey's gut tightened. She hadn't tried to get to know Mia, still too fresh from her own disappointing pregnancy test result. To hear that Mona was doing great caring for the infant drove it home to Audrey that she herself wasn't meant to be a mother. Perhaps she was better at helping the stray adults of the world find their place.

"What about you, Audrey? Why are you so helpful to others? Libby and Isabella have only nice things to say about you. You gave them jobs at the Ugly Stick Saloon when they didn't have anywhere else to go. Like me."

"Like them, I know what it feels like to be down and out. The man who used to own the Ugly Stick took pity on me and gave me a job. Now I own the place, I like to give back."

"You're a good person." Beth stared at the road ahead. "Just when I think there aren't any good ones left in the world." The last sentence she whispered almost too low for Audrey to hear. But she did.

"I've found that Temptation is full of good people. You just have to get to know them." When she pulled into the parking lot of the only grocery store in town, Audrey turned off the engine and reached out to touch Beth's wrist before she could get out.

Audrey said softly, "The men here are big, strong, and can be scary. But they have good hearts and wouldn't let anyone hurt the ones they love. That goes for the women too. If someone threatens you, let me know. I don't tolerate bullies."

Beth smiled, her bottom lip trembling. "Thanks. I won't forget."

Audrey shopped, following Beth without trying to be obvious about it. When she would pick up an item, check the price and put it back on the shelf, Audrey made note of it and came behind her, dropping it into her own cart.

Christmas music was piped through the speaker system, reminding her she hadn't completed her gift buying for her family and employees. Only three weeks left meant that she had to get on it soon.

With the limited amount of money Beth had from tips at the saloon, she purchased necessities like diapers, bottled water and formula, with enough left over for a jar of peanut butter, a loaf of bread, dry cereal and a quart of milk.

Audrey's heart ached for her. She'd been that down and out before and hated seeing anyone in the same dire straits. Making her own purchases, she helped load everything in the truck from hers and Beth's carts, while Beth strapped Mia in the car seat.

The trip back to the saloon was completed in a comfortable silence.

When they arrived at the trailer, Audrey carried bags in while Beth collected Mia and the car seat.

Mia woke up crying as Beth lifted her from the car seat. "Could you hold her while I get a bottle ready?"

Audrey took Mia in her arms and cradled her, rocking back and forth.

Mia stared up at her, her cries quieting.

"You're good with her," Beth said, filling the bottle with powder formula and water. "Are you and Jackson planning on having children?"

Audrey swallowed hard on the lump that rose in her throat. "Maybe."

"You'll make a great mother." Beth capped and shook the bottle to mix the powder in the water. "Do you want to feed her?"

Audrey nodded, taking the bottle from Beth. When she touched the nipple to the baby's lips, Mia opened her mouth. Soon the baby was happily gulping down the formula.

"These aren't my groceries." Beth stood at the dining table, picking through the bags Audrey had brought in.

"Yes, they are," Audrey insisted.

Beth frowned. "I didn't buy them." She pushed her shoulders back. "I won't accept charity."

"Don't call it charity. Call it a gift. Or maybe paying it forward. Someday, when you're firmly on your feet, you can help someone else out." Audrey glanced up from Mia and smiled. "Please. It makes me happy to help."

Beth's frown deepened. "You've already helped me so much. I'm using your electricity and water. You've given me a job."

"No. I don't give anyone a job. They work for it. And I've seen how hard you work. I'm lucky to have you." Audrey stared down at the baby. "And I can't have my staff going hungry and falling over on the barroom floor."

"I wasn't going hungry." The strength of Beth's argument dissipated. Finally, her shoulders sagged. "I knew it would be hard making it on my own. But I didn't realize just how hard it would be with a baby."

"That's why you have friends."

She snorted softly. "I haven't had friends since high school."

Audrey glanced up at the statement. Beth stared at the bags, tears welling in her eyes.

The more Audrey learned about Beth, the more convinced she was that Beth had been abused by her husband. Whether mentally or physically, she'd been abused. Based on the bruise she'd seen on Beth's temple the night Beth had arrived, Audrey suspected both types of abuse. She tipped Mia up and laid her across her shoulder like she'd seen Beth do.

The baby immediately burped.

"Here, I'll take her." Beth laid Mia on the bed. "She'll need a fresh diaper and then she'll sleep for a couple of hours."

Now that her arms were empty, Audrey grasped just how empty they were and would continue to be. She needed to get away from the mother and baby before she did something stupid, like cry. "I need to get back to town and do some Christmas shopping. Are you two going to be okay?"

Beth nodded. "Thanks to you."

Audrey pulled her key chain out of her pocket and slipped the key to the Ugly Stick Saloon off the ring. "If you need to use a phone, this is the key to the back door. I hate to think of you out here without a vehicle or the ability to call in the case of an emergency."

Beth took the key. "Are you sure? We only met a few days ago. You know nothing about me."

Audrey hugged the girl. "I have faith in my intuition. I sense you're trustworthy and you wouldn't do anything to harm me. Now take the key. I don't want you stranded if you or the baby should become ill."

"Thank you." Beth's eyes welled again and a tear slipped down her face. "I don't know why you're being so nice, but thanks." She hugged Audrey again.

Outside the trailer with the door closed behind her, Audrey almost went back inside to tell Beth she and Mia could stay with them until they got on their feet. But her promise to Jackson won out. The weather was supposed to stay fairly warm for the next couple of days. The camp trailer would be fine.

But come hell or high water, by Christmas, Beth and Mia would have a solid roof over their heads and floors without wheels beneath their feet.

CHAPTER FIVE

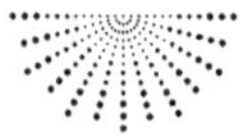

"I haven't seen the Ugly Stick Saloon this busy on a Thursday night since rodeo week." Libby wiped the bar down for the hundredth time since they'd opened that afternoon.

It was well past ten and none of the cowboys or cowgirls seemed in a hurry to leave to get ready for work the following day.

"I think with the holiday quickly approaching, everyone is getting into the Christmas spirit. Either they want to share in the fun or they don't want to be alone at this time of year," Audrey said. "Two weeks until Christmas. Holy cow. I haven't finished my shopping."

"I can't get over the change in Beth." Charli stood beside Audrey and nodded at the petite brunette with the flushed cheeks and happy smile as she served a table of cowboys mugs of beer. "You'd have thought someone had kicked her favorite dog when she came to work here. And now she's shines like a light bulb turned on."

"Beth seems to be coming out of her shell, and Mia has put on at least a pound since Mona started watching her in the evenings."

"When is Grant coming home?"

"Mona said he's on his way back from Vegas now. If they don't have any problems on the road, they'll be home tomorrow."

"Then what's Beth going to do for a sitter?"

"Mona wants to keep watching Mia. She's getting attached to that kid." Audrey completely understood. The baby was smiling now and she had the sweetest temperament. If Audrey were around her as much as Mona was, she'd fall in love with the baby as well. That's why she limited her visits to the trailer. The more she saw of the baby, the more she wanted to hold her and the deeper the ache in her belly.

Three weeks had flown by. The Ugly Stick Saloon had become party central. Every ranch and business in and around Temptation and Hole in the Wall, Texas wanted to schedule a party.

Audrey was glad for the business. It kept her too busy to mope about not having a baby of her own.

She and Jackson had backed off trying to get pregnant and settled back into their normal sex life where they had fun with each other, and it was all the more special because it wasn't calculated. He'd even asked her out to the barn to help with a newborn colt, only to trick her into making love on a blanket in the hay. Of course there was a riding crop and chaps to make it more fun.

Audrey smiled. She loved Jackson more than she loved breathing. He hadn't pressured her about babies and he'd brought her flowers every day, claiming it was part of his plan to surprise her at Christmas.

Her smile fading, Audrey remembered she still hadn't gotten Jackson anything. And by the number of bouquets of flowers he'd given her, he was probably planning something really special for her for Christmas morning.

This would be their first Christmas as a married couple. She had to make it special.

Mark and Luke sat at the bar, teasing Libby as she worked. Maybe they would know what Jackson would like.

Audrey marched over to the bar and squeezed in between her brothers-in-law.

"Hey, sis." Mark, ever the playful brother, grabbed her around the waist and planted her on his knee. "What's shaking?"

"I need help."

Luke's brow furrowed and he captured her hand in his. "Is the business in trouble? Jackson giving you hell? Are you sick?"

Audrey laughed. Luke was entirely too serious, but totally lovable. Libby had her hands full with the twins. They were so very different, but each loved her to distraction and she loved them too. "No, I'm okay, the business is okay and Jackson is all I could ever want in a husband."

"Then what's got your shorts in a wad?" Mark grinned. "Shoot. Luke and I can solve anything."

"What should I get for Jackson for Christmas? Solve that."

Luke and Mark spoke as one. "Everything but that."

Audrey frowned. "Do you mean to tell me you don't know your brother well enough to give me even a hint at what he'd like as a gift?"

"Oh, we know him all right," Luke said. "But the man has everything he could ever want and he'll be the first to tell you. He's got a ranch, enough money to be comfortable, family around him and you."

Audrey's heart filled with love for her younger brothers. "Thank you." She hugged Luke. "But there has to be something."

"A sexy nightgown?"

Audrey shook her head. "Bought one three weeks ago."

"A man can't have too many sexy nightgowns for his woman," Luke commented, his gaze on Libby.

Mark's eyes took on a devilish gleam and his focus turned to Libby as well. "Unless he prefers her naked." He said the words loud enough that Libby could hear.

"You two behave yourselves. I have to work another two hours before I can go with you two to Dallas to look at that stud."

"Speaking of studs, aren't you due a break?" Mark asked. "Or could you use a little help getting a case of something out of the storeroom?"

Libby rolled her eyes. "I've got everything I need up here. And my boss is listening."

With a laugh, Audrey hopped off Mark's lap. "I'll spell you for a few if you want to look for that case of missing Jack Daniels I never found three weeks ago."

Luke and Mark both left their bar stools in a shot. "We can help you lift the boxes."

"Are you sure?" Libby's face flushed an excited pink. "I don't mind working straight through, and I kinda wanted to leave a little early so that we can hit the road and not be dragging ass as we arrive at the outskirts of Dallas."

"I can mix a drink or two, and I don't mind if you leave a little early. Besides, these guys aren't likely to last long in the storeroom." Audrey winked.

Mark frowned. "Hey, you're attacking my manhood."

"Good." Luke hooked Libby's arm and turned her away. "While you're defending it, Libby and I will just make our way back to the storeroom and look for the case of whiskey."

"Not without me." Mark followed Luke and Libby down the hallway to the storeroom.

Audrey took Libby's place behind the bar and filled two drink orders for cowboys sitting on the stools.

"Those two weren't much help, were they?" Charli set her tray on the counter and gave Audrey her order.

While Audrey filled mugs and popped the tops off some longnecks, she lamented, "I have no clue what to get Jackson for Christmas."

"How about a battery-powered drill gun?"

"He has three."

"A set of socket wrenches. Nothing says love like a bunch of tools to a man."

"He has more tools than a man can ever use in a lifetime."

"A tool box?"

"He's got two." Audrey sighed. "I haven't got a clue what to get him."

"I bet he just wants to be surrounded by his family—you—with a home-cooked meal and a lit Christmas tree."

"I'm not much of a cook."

"There you go. If you put a little effort into it, you'll do great and he'll be so happy you made him feel special he won't care if you burn the whole damned meal."

"You think so?" Audrey stared at her assistant manager and friend. "I want him to know how much I love him."

"Honey, he knows." Charli stared across at where Jackson sat playing a friendly hand of poker with Connor Mason, Ed Judson and Nick McBride. "He's losing bad at his hand of poker because he can't quit looking at you."

"I'm surprised Connor's in the game. That's about the fifth time he's glanced up at you," Audrey pointed out.

"We are a couple of horny women, aren't we?"

"In love with a couple of horny men."

"And damn happy to be. I'd have blown this joint a long time ago if Connor hadn't shown me what fun we could have together." Charli lifted her tray filled with drinks. "Speaking of which, when will Mark, Luke and Libby be done in the storeroom?"

"Good grief. You'd think we were running a

bordello, not a saloon, with as much boinking as goes on in that storeroom."

Charli winked. "On second thought, I'd rather check out the costumes backstage with Connor."

"Hey, I can't run the bar and serve the tables at the same time."

With an over-exaggerated sigh Charli said, "I guess I could wait until closing. If I must. Although Connor's giving me that look."

Audrey laughed and went to work filling trays for Kendall and Lacey, too busy to think past the next drink. As she caught up, the telephone on the wall behind the bar rang. She turned to answer. "Ugly Stick Saloon, this is Audrey."

"Hey, Audrey, thank goodness I got you. It's Sam Whitefeather."

A stab of dread knifed through Audrey at Sam's intense tone. "What's wrong?"

"There's been an accident," he said.

Audrey gripped the phone tightly and strained to hear him over the noise in the bar. "Holy hell, Sam. Are you all right?"

"I am. Can you get a message to Mona?"

"Sure. What do you want to me to tell her?"

"Grant's in the hospital in Albuquerque, New Mexico. He got run off the road by an eighteen-wheeler and is pretty banged up."

"Oh, Sam. Is he going to be okay?"

"Yes, but he's asking for Mona. The doctor wants to keep him a couple days. He broke a few ribs, punctured his lungs and has a concussion. He won't be traveling for a couple days at least."

"I'll get the message to her right away."

"I can pick her up at the airport. Tell her to let me know when she arrives."

"I will. Are you sure you're okay?"

"I'm fine, just bruised. Luckily the horses are okay. Gotta go, the doctor is motioning for me."

"Take care, Sam." Audrey hung up as Libby returned from her break, all smiles and her face flushed a pretty pink.

As soon as she saw Audrey, her smile faded. "What's wrong?"

"Grant's been in an accident. I need to let Mona know." As she hurried toward the rear exit of the building, Audrey gave Libby the digest version of what happened. "Call Jake Maddox. He might be able to fly her out there on shorter notice than an airline."

Outside, the night air was cooler than Audrey remembered going in earlier. What had the weatherman said? The temperatures were expected to drop into the forties. She had to get Beth and Mia to move to the ranch house that night. The trailer had been warm enough, but she didn't want them taking the chance of running out of propane in the middle of the cold night.

Audrey walked up the metal steps, knocked on the door and waited.

"The door is unlocked," Mona called out.

Audrey entered as Mona stood with Mia in her arms. "About time you came out to see us. Mia's been wondering where her Aunt Audrey's been hiding." Mona nuzzled the baby. "Haven't you, sweetie?"

Audrey touched Mona's shoulder. "Mona, honey, Grant's been in an accident."

Mona's gaze shot to Audrey, the color leaching from her face. "Is he okay?"

"The doctor says he should be okay, but they're keeping him under observation in the hospital in Albuquerque for a few days. He's asking for you."

"I have to go." Mona handed Mia to Audrey and slipped the strap of her purse over her shoulder. "I need to catch a flight out of Abilene or Dallas, whichever leaves soonest."

Audrey tucked a blanket around Mia. "Touch base with Libby before you leave the saloon. I had her call Jake Maddox."

"Of Maddox Charters?" Mona shook her head. "I can't afford to fly charter. I'm a cosmetologist, not a millionaire."

"Jake's a friend of mine, and he owes me a favor. I'll get him to cut me a deal. Don't worry. I'll handle it. Now go." Holding Mia in her arms, Audrey herded Mona out of the trailer.

As Mona entered through the back door of the saloon, Audrey glanced down at Mia. "We better make that call to Jake so that he bills me, not Mona."

Audrey glanced around the tight confines of the trailer and spotted the infant car seat. Balancing the baby in one arm, she hooked the baby's seat on her elbow and eased through the narrow doorway and down the steps to the ground.

The air was a lot cooler than earlier. Much too cool for the baby. Audrey closed the trailer door and hurried into the saloon to her office, where she laid Mia in the car seat and sat her on the floor beside her, the desk effectively blocking anyone from tripping over the baby accidentally.

Audrey thumbed through her old-fashioned Rolodex until she found the Maddox Charters card she'd held on to since the time she'd saved Jake Maddox from a huge DUI ticket. He'd been on a bender after his fiancée stood him up at the altar. He'd been so stinking drunk he would have killed himself had he gotten behind the wheel of his truck.

Recognizing how drunk he was, Audrey had stolen his keys from him and locked him in her office until he slept off the effects of the alcohol.

The next morning, Jake had thanked her shame-facedly and left his card with his personal cell phone number on it. Sure, he owed her. But did he owe her enough to take Mona out to Albuquerque on really short notice?

Punching the numbers into the phone, she crossed her fingers and waited for Jake to answer.

JACKSON MUST HAVE GLANCED up a hundred times since he started the poker game with Connor, Nick and Ed.

"Are you going to play or sit there and stare at Audrey all night?" Ed asked.

"Sorry. Don't know what's wrong with me." Jackson

looked at his cards, selected three and laid them face down on the table. "I'll take three."

"You remember that red Corvette convertible I bought out of that barn auction?" Nick was saying.

"Yeah, it was in pretty bad shape when you got it," Connor said. "What did you do with it?"

"I spent a month of Sundays working on the engine and refurbishing the interior. I'm proud to say it's running like a song."

"With a good paint job, you'll have a nice piece of machinery," Ed said. "You gonna sell it?"

"As a matter of fact, the shop is getting so busy, I really don't have room for it. And now that the engine's running, I've kind of lost interest." Nick laid down two cards. "Hit me twice."

"Does that mean you're going to sell it?" Jackson asked.

"I have a paint shop lined up, but I don't know if I want to spend the money when I don't have a place to store it."

"Jackson..." Ed turned his way. "Didn't you drive a beat-up old Corvette in high school?"

Jackson nodded. "Seems like such a long time ago."

"What happened to it?"

"I traded it in on a truck for the ranch." Jackson stared at his cards, not seeing them, remembering that old car and the fun he'd had driving it. "I hated giving it up, but I needed the truck."

"Why don't you buy Nick's 'vette?" Connor suggested.

"What would I do with a Corvette?" Jackson asked. "I

own a ranch. A 'vette only has seating for two. In case you haven't heard, Audrey and I are trying to get pregnant. Where would I put a kid in a Corvette?"

"In the trunk?" Connor offered.

Jackson frowned at Connor. "Last I heard, putting kids in the trunk was illegal."

"You'll be trading your truck in for a minivan before you know it," Ed joked.

"If it makes Audrey happy, I'd do it."

"Still no luck?"

"No. And Audrey is getting so down about it."

"I'm sorry to hear that." Nick clapped a hand on Jackson's back. "If you need a place to hang around in with tools, come on down to the shop. I've got more work than I have time for."

"I might take you up on that."

"So I take it you're not interested in the Corvette?" Nick persisted.

Shaking his head, Jackson stared at the cards in his hand. "I'd love it, but it's not part of the game plan. And neither are these cards. Who shuffled?"

The other three men at the table answered as one, "You!"

"I guess my head's not in the game." Jackson glanced up, hoping to catch a glimpse of Audrey. He didn't see her behind the bar, so he scanned the saloon to see if she was waiting tables to give one of the waitresses a break. Though he didn't find her behind the bar or wading through the tables, he wasn't all too concerned.

When Mona turned up behind the bar and engaged

in an intense conversation with Libby, Jackson sat forward.

Beth was serving drinks. Mona was supposed to be watching Mia, and Audrey was nowhere to be seen.

Jackson tossed his cards on the table and stood. "Sorry, guys, I'm done for the night."

"I'm all in too." Connor tossed his cards onto Jackson's. "It's getting late and I have to work tomorrow."

"Me too." Nick stood and stretched.

Jackson left the others, heading for the bar. Before he reached it, Mona pushed past him and shot out the back of the building.

"What's going on?" Jackson asked.

Libby cleared a tray of empty mugs and loaded it with full ones. "Grant was in an accident out near Albuquerque. Mona is going to be with him."

"Where's Audrey?"

"With the baby, I assume." Libby went back to managing the bar as Jackson left for the back door.

When he stepped outside, a tall, dark shadow ducked around the side of the little trailer. Jackson had hauled the truck off to Nick McBride's shop the day before to have him reinstall the starter he'd pulled and to do a complete checkup on the rest of the engine.

"Hey!" Jackson called out.

The shadow emerged into the light, revealing a big, muscular man wearing dark jeans and a dark T-shirt.

"Can I help you with something?" Jackson asked.

The man tipped his head toward the trailer. "Yours?"

The hair on the back of Jackson's neck stood on end. Something about this guy rubbed Jackson wrong. First, what was he doing lurking around the back of the saloon? Jackson made a snap decision. "Yes," he lied. The man was a stranger. If he was moving on, the lie wouldn't mean anything. "Why do you ask?"

"Thought I'd seen it before. My in-laws had one just like it."

Jackson shrugged. "If you're looking for a drink, you'll have to go around to the front entrance of the building. This entrance is for authorized personnel only."

The man's eyes narrowed slightly. If Jackson hadn't been watching, he might have missed it in the yellow glow from the security light. "Thanks. I could use one."

Jackson waited for the man to walk around the side of the building, and then he gave it another ten seconds before he crossed the parking lot to the tiny trailer. The door was unlocked and the light was still on over the kitchen sink. Neither Mia nor Audrey were inside.

His heart beating a little faster, Jackson entered through the back door of the saloon, glanced in the backstage area and moved on to Audrey's office.

He burst through the door to find Audrey on the telephone.

She pressed a finger to her lips and motioned for him to close the door.

Jackson complied.

Audrey said, "Thank you so much, Jake. Now I owe you one." She hung up and turned to Jackson. "I suppose you heard about Grant?"

Jackson nodded. "What I want to know is who has Mia?"

Audrey touched a finger to her lips again and pointed to the floor beside her.

Leaning over the desk, Jackson could see the infant car seat with Mia sleeping peacefully inside. He let go of the breath he hadn't known he'd been holding and relaxed. "When I saw Mona in the bar, I knew something was up. Then the man lurking around the trailer made me worried."

A frown settled on Audrey's forehead. "What man?"

"I didn't recognize him as a local. He asked about the trailer."

Audrey's frown deepened. "What did you tell him?"

Jackson grinned. "I told him it was mine."

"And he bought it?"

"He didn't argue the point."

"Where is he now?"

"I told him if he wanted a drink, he had to enter the bar through the front door."

Audrey pushed to her feet. "Where's Beth?"

"Serving drinks."

Audrey lunged for the door.

Before she reached it, the door flew open and Beth threw herself through, slamming the door behind her. Her eyes wide and wild, her face white as a sheet, she flung herself into Audrey's arms. "Oh God. He's here."

"Who's here?"

"My husband, Randall Neal." She let go of Audrey. "I have to get Mia."

Audrey set Beth to the side. "Calm down. Mia's safe behind my desk." Audrey nodded toward Jackson.

He reached for the lock on the door and twisted it as a solid knock sounded.

Beth pressed her fist to her mouth, a sound like a wounded animal rising up her throat. "He can't find us. I can't go back to that," she whispered.

"It's okay. Get in my closet. Jackson and I will handle this." Audrey guided Beth to her closet. "Just a minute," she called out loud enough whoever was at the door could hear her over the music in the bar.

As Audrey closed the door to the closet, Beth put out her hand to stop her. "What about Mia?"

"She's hidden behind my desk. Don't worry." Audrey closed the door, untied her shirt, unbuttoned the top button on her shorts and ruffled her hair. "Kiss me," she told Jackson.

He did, his body's response instant, his cock pushing against the fly of his jeans.

Another knock on the door made him step back and he unbuttoned the top button of his jeans and the buttons down the front of his shirt.

With a brief nod from Audrey, he opened the door to the man he'd met out in the back parking area.

"Oh, it's you again." He gave the man an irritated glare. "We're busy in here, if you don't mind."

"I'm sorry to interrupt." The man's lip curled up on one side in a sneer as he glanced past Jackson to Audrey. "The girl tending bar told me to ask you if you'd seen this woman." He held up a photograph of a woman with bleached-blond hair and a heart-shaped face. Though the photo was slightly blurred, Jackson couldn't mistake the face. It was Beth.

Jackson leaned over the photo and pretended to consider it. "Nope. Can't say that I have." He looked up. "Who is she?"

"Elizabeth Neal. My wife," the man ground out between clenched teeth. "She ran out on me and took my baby with her." He stared past Jackson.

Audrey tied her shirt beneath her breasts and looked over Jackson's shoulder. "Haven't seen that woman. If we do, who should we contact?"

"Me. Randall Neal." He dug a card out of his wallet and handed it to Jackson.

"Why would she run?" Jackson asked.

Randall's eyes narrowed. "How the hell should I know? Maybe it's postpartum depression or she's just fucked in the head. All I want is what's mine back where they belong."

Jackson's hands balled into fists and he had to fight to keep from slugging the man for the crappy way he talked about his wife and baby daughter. He'd bet good money this guy wasn't above hitting a woman, thus explaining the bruise on Beth's temple the day she'd showed up at the bar. And that was probably why Beth was hiding in the closet, afraid to come out.

"If you don't mind. My wife and I were in the middle of something." Jackson started to close the door.

Randall stuck his foot in the gap. "If you see her, tell her that I'll find her. I keep what's mine." The man removed his foot.

Before Jackson could close the door, Mia gave a soft, bleating cry.

Randall's palm slapped the door. "What was that?"

Audrey squealed and giggled. "Stop that, honey. Wait until you close the door all the way."

"Can I help it you're hot in those shorts?" He poked her side and she squealed again, slapping his hand away.

Randall glared at them as Jackson closed the door and locked it.

They waited, listening for the sound of footsteps walking away. Jackson held his breath, anger burning so hot he wanted to slam through the door and tell the man exactly what he thought of him. But he didn't. If he revealed that he knew Beth, Randall might barge in and demand Beth and the baby be turned over to him.

At that point, Jackson would have to kill the man.

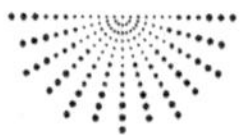

CHAPTER SIX

Audrey opened the closet door and Beth fell into her arms, sobbing.

"It's no use. We'll never be safe. Randall will always find us." Beth's shoulders shook as Audrey held her.

"We won't let him hurt you." Audrey stroked her back as if Beth was a distraught child.

"What if he gets a court order to have Mia taken away from me? He can pull strings. He knows all the judges. They trust him!"

Audrey stared over her shoulder at Jackson as she murmured words of reassurance. "It'll be all right. He can't do that."

"I don't know, babe." Jackson held up Randall's card. "The man's a prosecuting attorney. He might have some clout in the court system."

"He does. I couldn't tell anyone he was…hurting me. No one would have believed me. Randall has every cop in Austin batting on his team. He's considering running for election to the US Senate. You heard him. He'll tell everyone I've gone off the deep end with postpartum depression." Her jaw tightened. "The irony is that I've never been clearer in my mind than after I delivered Mia. I won't let her grow up in the hell I've lived in for the past six years."

"So it's true? Your husband abused you?" Audrey held her tighter, her heart breaking for the young woman. Having been in an abusive relationship, Audrey knew how hard it was to leave.

Beth bowed her head, tears streaming down her cheeks. "I couldn't do anything right. If I spilled something, he hit me. If I didn't fold his shirts right, he hit me. If he was in a bad mood because he'd lost one of his cases, he hit me." Beth pushed the dark hair back from damp face. "At one point I had so many bruises I couldn't leave the house for two weeks. I got to where I didn't want to leave the house. I thought it was because I wasn't good enough."

Her chest squeezing tight, Audrey pushed Beth to arm's length and smoothed the hair out of her face. "Oh, sweetie, life is not supposed to be that hard."

"Then I got pregnant," Beth continued. "And he was so sweet and nice, and for nine months he didn't hurt me. He was ecstatic about the baby. His campaign manager said it would help him with the election. I thought he was changing; he was so very careful not to hurt the baby growing inside of me." Her voice grew more ragged with each word. Beth paused before continuing. "The night I went into labor, he was angry with me for waking him. It wasn't time, he said. He had a big case the next day and needed his sleep. I tried to be quiet, but it hurt so bad and the pain was only getting worse. I drove myself to the hospital."

"Oh, Beth." Audrey hugged her. "I'm so sorry. I wish I could have been there for you."

"Randall was angry when he realized I'd gone. His campaign manager wanted pictures of him with his newborn baby to go on the front page of the paper. All I wanted was to make sure Mia was okay. She was too early. They thought her lungs might not be fully developed. Randall insisted on holding her when she should have been in the NICU. I begged him to let the doctors and nurses do their jobs.

"But he wanted that damned picture and made Mia wait until the cameraman dragged himself to the hospital twenty minutes later. Mia was struggling to breathe by then.

"Once the photo was taken, Mia was wheeled to the NICU and everyone cleared out of my room, Randall slapped me for making such a fuss." Beth straightened, pushing her shoulders back. "I swore then that I wouldn't live that way anymore. When I was strong enough, and Beth was well enough to travel, I loaded my parents' old camp trailer and truck with everything I could sneak out of the house, and I left. I was going to drive all the way to Mexico when I ran out of gas and money here at the Ugly Stick Saloon."

"I'm glad you made it this far," Audrey said.

"Me too. But now that he's found me, you and Jackson could go to jail for harboring me. If I know

Randall, he'll throw every lawsuit he can dream up at you two. The best thing I can do is leave."

"No." Audrey shook her head. "You can't keep running. Mia needs a place to call home and you need to be where you feel safe."

"I can't let him ruin your lives like he's ruining mine."

"He won't. And you're moving in with us so we can protect you." Audrey put her arm around Beth's shoulders. "Come on. We're taking you and Mia to the Gray Wolf Ranch. You'll be safe there."

"I can't. You two have already done enough. I won't accept any more of your charity."

"If you won't do it for you, do it for Mia," Jackson insisted.

"You two are newlyweds. Mia and I would be in your way."

"We have our whole lives to be newlyweds. You need us now, and we won't take no for an answer." Audrey gripped Beth's arms gently. "You deserve happiness for all the horror you've put up with."

"It's only a matter of time before he finds out where I am," Beth warned. "When he does, he'll launch an attack, either legal or physical. No. I can't do this." She pulled out of Audrey's embrace. "You two are nice people. I won't let Randall cause problems for you."

"At least stay with us until we can find a safe location for you. I'm sure Jackson knows someone who has a place you can hide out at until Randall gives up and leaves the area."

Beth hesitated, chewing her bottom lip. She sighed.

"Okay. But just for the night. The trailer won't be safe. He's seen it and knows I'm around here somewhere. For all I know, he's watching it now. Waiting for me to return."

"If he's still here…" Jackson walked to the office door, "…I can distract him while you three make a break for it. Go to the ranch and stay there. Lock the doors and load the pistol I gave you for your birthday. I'll be right behind you as soon as you've had enough of a head start."

"Thanks, babe." Audrey kissed Jackson on the lips. "You're the best."

Beth wiped the tears from her eyes. "You're a lucky woman, Audrey."

"I know."

Jackson paused with his hand on the doorknob. "Stay behind the door and lock it as soon as I walk out. I'll send Charli back to give you the all-clear once I have Neal engaged in conversation."

"Be careful and don't let him have much alcohol," Beth said. "He's a mean drunk."

Jackson winked. "I can take care of myself. You two take care of yourselves and Mia."

"We will," Audrey concurred.

Jackson cracked the door and peered out into the hallway. Then he slipped through.

Audrey locked the door behind him, leaned against it and stared at the pale young woman in front of her. Her heart ached at how much she'd had to suffer. "You'll be okay. I promise."

"He's far too smart." Beth wrung her hands, her

brow furrowed in a worried frown. "Taking me and Mia into your home will only bring you more trouble."

"We can handle it." Audrey put on a good show, but she'd feel a whole lot better when she had her .40-caliber pistol loaded and ready to take on any trespasser at the Gray Wolf Ranch.

Beth lifted Mia into her arms and rocked her while Audrey paced the room.

After what seemed like an hour but was only about fifteen minutes, a soft knock came. "Audrey, it's me, Charli."

Audrey leaned her cheek against the door. "Are you alone?"

"Yes," Charli's voice sounded through the door panel.

Audrey opened it a crack.

Charli glanced over her shoulder. "Jackson has the bastard occupied. Let's get you two out the back door while the going is good. Greta Sue and I will stand guard at the end of the hallway. We won't let anyone past."

Beth laid Mia in the car seat and adjusted the straps around her.

"Let me carry her." Audrey hooked her elbow through the handle and handed Beth her keys. "Go ahead of me and open the truck doors."

Charli and Greta Sue blocked the end of the hallway, staring out at the bar. Charli turned and nodded, mouthing the word *Hurry.*

"Go." Audrey gave Beth a gentle nudge.

Beth shot out into the hall, glancing toward the bar, her eyes wide and wary.

Audrey followed, carrying Mia in the car seat.

They made it out the back of the building and to Audrey's truck without encountering any problems. The two minutes it took for Audrey to buckle the car seat into the back of the truck were two of the longest minutes of Audrey's life. Beth took those two minutes to race through the trailer, grabbing everything she and the baby would need.

When she returned to the truck, Beth dumped her stuff on the back floorboard and climbed in the passenger side.

Audrey slipped into the driver's seat of her red pickup. As she reversed out of her parking space, Charli burst through the back door and waved her down.

Audrey hit the automatic window button and it slid down.

"He's leaving the bar," Charli called out, breathing hard.

Beth pressed a hand to her mouth, fear in her eyes.

"Duck down in the seat," Audrey commanded.

Beth bent forward as Audrey drove around the side of the saloon.

A man emerged from the bar and stared at her truck as she passed by. She pretended not to notice him, but she watched in her peripheral vision as he climbed into a car and backed out.

Audrey pressed her foot to the accelerator and sped toward Temptation, hoping to get far enough ahead of Randall to lose him. Once she reached Temptation, she zigzagged through the streets, glancing back often through her rearview mirror. She didn't see any headlights, so she finally headed out of town toward the ranch.

"You can straighten. No one is following us," she said.

Beth sat up and glanced over her shoulder at the road behind her and at Mia sleeping quietly. "I have a bad feeling about this."

"Don't." Audrey had been thinking through all the people she knew or had contacts with. "I have an attorney friend in Dallas who specializes in divorce. I'm going to call him as soon as we get to the ranch. If I'm not mistaken, he has some friends in high and low places. He can help you file the papers you need to start divorce proceedings."

"Randall will kill me." Beth shook her head. "This will ruin his chances at office."

"Do you want to stay married to a man who beats you?"

"No."

"Do you want to risk him hurting Mia?"

"No."

"Then let me put you in contact with Clayton Chance."

"Clayton Chance?" Beth's eyes widened. "The high-power divorce attorney who helped that computer CEO through his breakup with the actress?"

"Yeah, that Chance." Audrey grinned. "They don't call him the Shark for nothing."

"I can't afford him."

"You won't have to. He'll have your ex paying all his fees."

"I wish I had your confidence."

"Honey, I used to be where you are. Then I got tired of being pushed around. I suspect you're tired of it too. And, as you said, Mia deserves a better life."

Audrey pulled through the arched gate of the Gray Wolf Ranch and along the driveway to the sprawling ranch house, where she shifted into park. "We're home."

Beth carried Mia inside while Audrey unloaded the items she'd brought from the trailer.

After settling Mia and Beth in one of the guest bedrooms, Audrey got on the phone to Clayton Chance, cringing at the lateness of the hour.

"Audrey?" Clayton's voice came over the line hoarse and groggy. "Are you all right?"

"I'm fine, Clayton." She didn't waste time, but launched into the purpose of the late call. "I need your expertise as the meanest divorce lawyer in town."

"Oh, sweetheart, are you and your Kiowa cowboy in trouble? I thought you said he was *the one*."

"We aren't and he is. I need your help for a friend of mine in an abusive situation. Her husband has some political pull in Austin. She needs someone who will cut through that crap and get her and her baby out of a bad environment for good."

"Sounds interesting. What's in it for me?"

Audrey smiled into the phone. "How about I provide the strippers for your bachelor party? Hell, I'll even host it at the Ugly Stick Saloon."

"Not much of a deal for me. I'll never marry, thus no bachelor party."

Audrey chuckled. "Clayton, you're a cynic."

"You've got that right. When you work in my field, it's hard to be anything else."

"I've been a cynic but found it to be self-defeating. I learned to never say never."

"Then you were never a true cynic."

"Will you help my friend or not?" Audrey asked.

"I'll help, and the best part is, you won't owe me a thing."

"I'll owe you that bachelor party," she said. "Be looking for a call from Beth Neal. And Clayton?"

"Yes, Audrey?"

"Your true love is out there. You just have to let her in."

"And you, my dear Audrey, are an optimist soon to be disappointed."

Audrey shook her head as she set the phone on the charger, scribbled Clayton's number on a piece of paper and found Beth mixing formula in the kitchen.

"Clayton is expecting your call. He has more pull in DC than the president himself. If anyone can get you that divorce and a restraining order, it's Clayton Chance."

Beth measured powder formula in a scoop and poured it carefully into a baby bottle. "Thank you. I'll call him first thing in the morning." She poured water on top of it, capped it with a nipple and a seal and shook the liquid until all the powder dissolved. "I'm worried what Randall will do when he finds out I'm here."

"The only people who know you're here are Jackson, Charli, you and I. None of us will tell Randall."

"But I have to work. If he sticks around long enough, he'll find me at the Ugly Stick."

"Then you can work here. I've told Jackson I need a housekeeper. This place is too big for the two of us to keep up with when we both have our own work to do."

Beth's shoulders sagged. "I feel like I've been nothing but trouble since I got here."

"No, sweetie, you and Mia are a joy. Let us help you. 'Tis the season, right?" Audrey chewed on her lip and made a decision. "As a matter of fact, we have just the place for Mia. Come." She grabbed Beth's hand and led her down the hall to the room she and Jackson had been working on for the past six months.

Her hand gripped the doorknob, and she pushed back her own disappointment over not getting pregnant, knowing this was the right thing to do. Then she flung the door open and flipped the light switch on.

Beth's mouth dropped open as she stepped into the room. "This is a baby's room."

Audrey studied the room through Beth's reaction, knowing how special it was and that it was perfect for Mia. Two walls were painted a pastel green, another a periwinkle bluish purple and the last wall a pale yellow. A shiny new mahogany-stained crib stood in one corner, decked out in a bed ruffle, sheets and bumper pads in the same purple and green of the paint on the walls.

"It's beautiful." Already Beth was shaking her head. "I can't. This room is special."

"It's the old nursery."

"You can't tell me the furnishings and linens are old.

It's move-in ready. All it needs is a…" Beth turned to Audrey, her eyes softening. "All it needs is a baby."

Audrey nodded. "Since Jackson and I can't seem to have one of our own, Mia can use the room."

"Oh, Audrey. I didn't know you two were trying." Beth touched her arm. "It must be hard having me and Mia around."

"At first. But now I'm growing to accept that I might not have children. I can spoil my friends' children. Starting with Mia."

Beth hugged Audrey and whispered, "Don't give up. It will happen for you. You and Jackson will make great parents."

Audrey fought back the tears that seemed to be around all too often lately. "Even if we don't have children, we have each other." She stepped away from Beth and glanced at her watch, frowning. "Speaking of which. Where is Jackson?"

Lights shone through the gaps around the window blinds.

Audrey and Beth emerged from the baby room as the front door opened and Jackson called out, "Where's my woman?"

"That's my cue." Beth smiled. "I'll just jump in the shower while Mia's asleep. That'll give you and Jackson some time alone."

Audrey smiled, rounded the corner and fell into her husband's arms. "Took you long enough."

"I followed Randall to a hotel in Temptation. I stuck around for half an hour to make certain he wasn't going out again. When he hadn't come out of his room by midnight, I decided it was clear and came on home."

"Thanks, babe." Audrey leaned up on her toes and kissed his lips.

"Where's Beth and Mia?"

Audrey laid a hand on Jackson's chest. "They're safe. Beth is getting a shower. I gave her the guest room. Mia will be staying beside her in the nursery."

Jackson's hands tightened around her. "Are you sure?"

"I've never been more certain. That nursery was meant for a baby. I'd rather use it than keep it as a shrine to something that might not happen."

"I haven't given up. And the nursery is not a shrine." Jackson smiled down at her. "But I'm glad you let Mia stay in there. We can help Beth with midnight feedings. The poor girl has to be exhausted."

Audrey nodded. "Yeah. I imagine she is."

Jackson tucked a strand of Audrey's hair behind her ear. "Are you sure you're okay with all this?"

Audrey wrapped her arms around his neck. "I am. And I gave her the number to Clayton Chance."

"I'd forgotten you knew him. If anyone can get her out of marriage to Randall, it's Clayton."

"Right." Audrey tipped his head down and stood on her toes to kiss him again. "Let's lock up and get to bed."

"You don't have to ask me to go to bed more than once, sweetheart. I haven't forgotten that I have the most beautiful wife in the world."

"Damn right you do. When Beth's out of the shower, I plan on taking a nice long hot one." She stepped out of his arms and turned toward their bedroom. "Don't be long locking up." With a wink, she entered their bedroom, unbuttoning her blouse. It slipped over her shoulders and fell to the ground behind her. Audrey shot Jackson a sultry look. He wouldn't be far behind.

He'd be extra quick and thorough locking all the doors and checking the latches on the windows, which would give her just enough time to pull back the covers on the bed, lay out fresh towels and get completely naked.

As she turned down the blankets, the phone on the nightstand rang. In Audrey's experience, late-night phone calls were never harbingers of good news. The caller ID on the digital display indicated the county sheriff's department.

Her gut clenching, Audrey grabbed up the phone, worried that one of her employees or saloon patrons had been involved in a wreck.

"This is Audrey," she said, her tone shakier than she'd intended.

"And Jackson. I'm on the other line." His voice came through the short distance, reassuring her that she had backup.

"Hey, you two, it's Deputy Cramer. I have some bad news."

Audrey sat on the side of the bed, her stomach churning.

Cramer went on. "That little trailer that was parked behind the Ugly Stick is lit up like a bonfire on the Fourth of July."

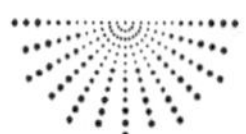

CHAPTER SEVEN

"I'm going with you," Audrey insisted, slinging her purse over her shoulder and grabbing her truck keys. She stood in the front entrance while Jackson stuffed his wallet and keys into his pockets, a stubborn frown wrinkling her brow. God, she was sexy when she was worried.

"You can't." Jackson gripped her arms and spoke in a low, insistent tone, trying to keep Beth from hearing all the commotion. "You heard Cramer. The fire department has it under control and they're keeping it from damaging the saloon."

"But I need to be there. It's my bar."

"Yeah, and it might be dangerous. Neal might still be hanging around. If both of us go, who will keep an eye on Beth and Mia?"

Audrey chewed on her lower lip. "Damn, I hate it when you're right."

"I need you to stay here and protect her. For that matter, maybe I should stay here too."

"No. One of us needs to be at the saloon in case they need to get inside."

"You could call Charli."

"No. It needs to be one of us." Audrey fiddled with her keys. "Maybe you should stay here and protect Beth and I should go."

"I don't like the idea of you being on the road with that maniac out there."

"Same goes for me."

"I'll go. You stay. Get that .40-caliber pistol I gave you for your birthday out and load it."

"You think he'll come here?"

"I don't know. But I'll put in a call to Mark and Luke and see if they can come by and stay the night, just in case."

Audrey shook her head. "They aren't there, remember? They left for Dallas when Libby got off work to look at that stud stallion they were considering for their stable. They won't be back until tomorrow night."

"Then I won't be gone long. Keep that gun handy."

"Gun?" Beth appeared in the hallway, her face pale, her long dark hair wet and slicked back from her face, making her appear even younger and more fragile.

"You explain." Jackson leaned over and kissed Audrey. "I'll be back as soon as possible." As he burst through the front door, he could hear Beth in the hallway.

"What's going on? Why's Jackson leaving when he just got here?"

The door closed behind him and the lock clicked in place.

Jackson hopped into his truck and spun gravel as he left the house and drove back to Temptation and through to the other side, where the night sky was lit up with an orange glow from the flames. His heart thumped against his ribs as he neared the Ugly Stick Saloon. From a distance, it appeared as if the saloon was on fire. Fire trucks, sheriff's vehicles and an ambulance lined the road, along with the personal vehicles of the county's volunteer firefighters.

Though the firemen had kept the fire from razing the saloon, a grass fire had sprung up around the area and was quickly spreading back toward town.

Jackson parked on the paved road and leaped out of his truck, running toward the center of the emergency personnel.

Rather than interrupt the command and control team working the incident, he found Deputy Cramer standing near the charred remains of the tiny trailer.

"What happened?" Jackson asked.

"From what we can tell, someone doused the trailer in an accelerant and set it on fire shortly after the bar closed."

"Damn."

"Fortunately, I was on my way back from Hole in the Wall and saw the flames. Thankfully, the wind was blowing away from the building. I was able to hold back the flames from the saloon until the fire department arrived. A couple times the wind shifted, sending the embers and flames pretty darned close to the structure.

If there hadn't been a water hose outside, there wouldn't have been an Ugly Stick anymore."

Jackson patted Cramer on the back. "Thanks, man. I don't know what Audrey would have done if her business was destroyed."

"That's why we have insurance," the deputy said. He glanced at Jackson. "Any idea who would do this?"

"I have a suspicion."

"I take it Miss Smith was the target."

Jackson nodded.

"We determined there were no occupants trapped inside. But if she wasn't inside, where is she? Please tell me she wasn't abducted."

"No. We took her to our place to keep her safe. Her estranged husband paid a visit to the Ugly Stick earlier this evening."

Deputy Cramer's brow dipped. "Wish you would have told me. I'd have kept an eye on him for you."

"We had no idea he was this dangerous."

"I'm surprised Audrey didn't come with you. I thought for sure she'd want to be here to protect her interests."

"She stayed with Beth and the baby at the ranch."

"Are your brothers out at the ranch with the ladies?"

"No, they're in Dallas."

Cramer stared into Jackson's eyes. "You mean no one is out there with them?"

"Audrey has a gun and she knows how to use it. And I didn't plan on staying too long here."

"Seems like a big fire for a little trailer." The deputy shook his head.

As Cramer spoke, the impact of his words hit Jackson in the gut. "God, I'm an idiot. He set this fire as a diversion." Jackson spun and ran back toward his truck.

Cramer called, "I'm right behind you."

Jackson didn't slow until he reached his truck. He threw open the door and jumped in. Grabbing his cell phone, he cursed at the lack of service. Jerking the shift into drive, he turned his truck around in the middle of the road and raced back the way he'd come, praying he wouldn't be too late.

The odds weren't too terrible with two women against one man. But if Neal wanted Beth bad enough, he might kill anyone standing in his way. That someone would be Audrey.

Jackson's pulse hammered against his veins and pounded in his ears.

Please don't hurt Audrey.

Audrey turned off all the living room lights and stood by the front window, staring out into the night.

"He's coming. I can feel it." Beth rubbed her arms in the darkness.

A cold draft rippled across the back of Audrey's neck. She felt it too. Though she had her gun, she couldn't be prepared for everything. Turning to Beth, she said softly, "Get Mia and put her in the master bedroom closet. Hide her behind whatever you can: shoes, blankets, long dresses, overcoats. Whatever you find that looks like it belongs. Hide with her and don't come out until Jackson or I tell you to."

Beth shook her head. "I can't let you face him alone. He's mean. You have no idea what he's fully capable of when he's angry."

Audrey laid her free hand on Beth's arm. "Just do it. If he shows up demanding to see you, I can tell him you're not here. Now go. If he's close, we don't want him to catch sight of you or the gig will be up. Hurry."

Beth ran down the hallway to the nursery.

Audrey remained at the window, standing guard, straining her eyes to see into the darkness surrounding the rambling ranch house.

She heard Beth's footsteps crossing the hallway into the master bedroom, but she didn't turn away from the window.

Something dark moved on the edge of the yard. The wind had picked up and tree branches swayed, causing the shadows to undulate. For a moment Audrey thought perhaps the movement was a product of her overly sensitized imagination. But when a dark form moved again, closer this time, swinging around to the back of the house, she knew it wasn't just her imagination. Someone was out there, and he wasn't coming to pay a friendly visit.

When the intruder disappeared around the side of the house, Audrey left her position at the front window and worked her way around, peering through whatever windows were on the side he'd disappeared to. When she reached the kitchen, moonlight streamed in through the window over the sink and the window in the back door.

Audrey hugged the shadows, her stomach churning and her heart racing. She fought to keep the food she'd eaten earlier down. Now was not the time to throw up. The hand holding the gun shook. She'd never shot anyone before. But she had no doubt that if Randall broke into the house, she'd pull the trigger. The bastard would not hurt Beth and Mia.

Firming her grip on the gun, Audrey waited, her back pressed against the wall. Nothing moved to block the moonlight shining in. She prayed Beth remained hidden in the master bedroom and that the baby didn't wake and cry out.

Jackson, hurry back. Audrey realized that all her heartache and depression from not getting pregnant meant nothing compared to what was in her heart now. She loved Jackson more than life. And if he did return to the house, she hoped Randall didn't get spooked and hurt him.

The sharp sound of glass shattering came from the back of the house, in the direction of the master bedroom, breaking through Audrey's musings.

She left her post in the kitchen, her breath catching in her throat as she ran toward the bedroom, holding her gun in front of her.

Please, Beth, stay hidden.

She rounded the corner into the bedroom and her gaze shot to the window beside the bed. The curtain billowed out when the wind caught it through the gaping hole in the cracked glass.

A rock lay on the floor at Audrey's feet, but the hole in the window wasn't large enough for anyone to get through.

Audrey held the gun like she had when she'd tested for her concealed carry license: her arms out front, one hand cupping the other, her finger on the trigger, safety off, waiting.

Nothing moved outside the window.

Was he playing with her?

She didn't dare get closer to the window. If he was armed, he could easily shoot her, and Beth would be defenseless.

Crouching low, she eased around to the unbroken window and nudged the curtain to the side. Nothing moved in the darkness.

A crash of glass sounded from the kitchen, and more sounds of breaking glass followed.

Damn. He'd done it again, diverting her attention away from his real purpose.

Audrey ran back through the house, pulse pounding, pushing back her fear to deal with the situation.

As she reached the entrance to the kitchen, a dark form dressed all in black with a ski mask pulled over his head and face leaped out, grabbed her wrist and jerked it upward, gun and all.

She pulled the trigger, the bullet ripping through the ceiling. Plaster and dust rained down on her, blinding her eyes. "Let go of me, you bastard!" she yelled, kicking out with her red boots, her toe connecting with the man's shins.

He banged her hand against the wall. The gun sailed

from her grip and clattered against the wood flooring. Unarmed, out-muscled, angry and afraid, Audrey fought like a wildcat.

The man backhanded her, his knuckles connecting with her cheekbone, shooting pain making her squeeze her eyes shut. Shoving her off balance, he flung her around by the arm, yanking it up behind her back. When his arm crossed her neck, Audrey knew she was in big trouble.

He tightened his hold, cutting off her air. "Where is she?" he growled in her ear. "Where's Elizabeth?"

"I…don't…know…who you're…talking about," Audrey gasped out.

"You damn well do." He pushed her arm up behind her back harder until the pain brought tears to her eyes. She refused to let one drop fall, even if the bastard broke her arm.

"Where is she?" he repeated.

"Who?"

"Elizabeth and my baby."

Fighting for air, she whispered, "Not here."

"I know she's here. I saw you leave with her."

"Left town," Audrey managed.

"Then you must be alone, and no one will miss you if I kill you now." He squeezed his arm around her throat, lifting her off the ground. "Elizabeth, I'm going to kill her if you don't come out!" he shouted.

Gray fog crept in at the edge of Audrey's vision. She tried to remain alert, but she was failing miserably. She'd failed Beth and Mia. And she would never see

Jackson's sweet face again. The fight leached out of her, and she sagged against the man.

The light blinked on.

"Let go of her, Randall. I'll go with you." The sound of Beth's voice carried to Audrey as if from the end of a long, dark tunnel.

The arm around her throat eased slightly.

Audrey gulped in air, while squiggly lines danced across her vision.

"Where's the baby?" Randall demanded.

"I left her at the babysitter's. We can go pick her up on the way home." Beth stood with her shoulders bowed, her head dipped and her gaze on Audrey. "Don't hurt my friend or I won't go with you."

"You'll go with me no matter what I do. She had no right to take you from me."

"She didn't take me from you." Beth's shoulders straightened. "I left."

His arm tightened again around Audrey's throat. "You're mine. You had no right to leave."

Beth's eyes widened as she stared across at Audrey. "You're right. I'll go with you now. Just let go of Audrey."

Randall hesitated, and then he flung Audrey across the room.

She bounced against the wall and collapsed in a heap on the floor, her head pounding, her vision slowly clearing. "Don't, Beth. He'll hurt you."

"Stay out of it, bitch!" He kicked her hard, his boot connecting with her hip.

Beth grabbed his arm. "Don't hurt her!"

Her husband backhanded her hard, the ring on his finger cutting her cheekbone. She sailed across the floor like a rag doll, hit the wall and slid down, her eyes filling with tears.

Anger pushed out the pain and Audrey lurched to her feet.

Randall punched her in the face and she went down, stars exploding in her head. When she could see straight again, headlights shone across the entrance hallway. Jackson was home. She scanned the floor for her fallen gun.

Randall's gaze followed hers and he lunged for the weapon.

Audrey kicked out, catching his shin, tripping him. He waved his hands in the air but hit the ground face-first.

Audrey scrambled across the wood flooring, snatched the gun and rolled onto her back as Randall pushed up to his hands and knees. "Move a muscle and I'll shoot your ass."

CHAPTER EIGHT

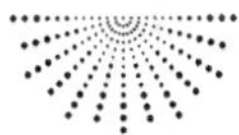

Randall froze, his eyes narrowing. "You won't shoot me."

"Oh yeah?" She leveled the gun on him, her hands shaking, her vision barely focused. "Try me."

For the first time in her life, Audrey wanted to kill a man. She waited for him to move, even to bat an eyelash. "Give me a reason to kill you. You're a coward and a son of a bitch. You don't deserve to be married to a woman as kind and bighearted as Beth."

"Fuck you," Randall spat at her. "Elizabeth is my wife. She belongs to me."

"Women aren't cattle to be owned. They're people who have the right to choose who they want to be with."

Randall glared at Beth, who sat cowering against the wall where she'd landed. "Tell her you want to be with me."

Beth's eyes widened and she glanced from Randall to Audrey and back to Randall. After a long pause, her eyes narrowed and she said in a low, clear tone, "I don't ever want to see you again. You're a bastard. As soon as I can, I'm divorcing you and I'm suing for sole custody of my daughter."

Audrey's chest swelled at the steel in Beth's tone and she faced Randall. "That settles it. You're done."

"Bitch!" He took a step forward.

Audrey raised the gun, pointing it at his chest. "You're pushing your luck."

"I'm going to push a lot more than that." He took another step.

Audrey pointed at the man's foot and pulled the trigger. The .40-caliber HK barely jerked in her hand, the bullet piercing the wooden floor an inch from Randall's foot.

He jumped back and snarled. "You'll pay for that."

"No. *You* will if you don't back off." It was only a matter of seconds before Jackson reached the house. If she could hold Randall off until he arrived, they'd put the jerk away for good.

"Audrey!" Jackson called out through the wooden front door. He pounded against it and rattled the handle.

For a split second, Audrey glanced toward the front of the house.

Randall took advantage of that momentary lapse in her attention and dove through the back exit at the same time Jackson broke down the front door.

"Audrey!" Jackson yelled, storming through the house.

"I'm in here." She pushed to her feet as Jackson entered the kitchen.

One look at her face and Jackson's cheeks burned a ruddy red, his lips curling back from his teeth in a fierce snarl. "Where is he?"

"He ran out the back door."

When Jackson hurled himself toward the exit, Audrey reached out to snag his arm.

"Don't go," she begged.

Jackson shoved her hand aside. "I'm going to kill him."

Audrey reached out again and hooked his elbow. "Please. Don't go." She fell against him, too tired and bruised to stand another minute.

Jackson caught her in his arms and scooped her up. "We can't let him get away with what he's done."

Deputy Cramer burst through the front door and ran straight through to where they were in the kitchen, skidding to a halt, breathing hard. "Damn, Jackson, you drove like a bat out of hell."

"Neal was here." Jackson jerked his head toward the broken back door. "He went out the back way. Stop him if you can."

"On it." Cramer ran through the kitchen, his weapon drawn. "I have backup on the way," he called over his shoulder.

Jackson started after him, still carrying Audrey.

Audrey cupped his cheek and turned his face to hers. "Let the authorities handle it. This time we have witnesses to what he's done. He won't get away with it."

She struggled against his hold. "Let me down. Beth's hurt and we need to check on Mia."

Jackson eased her to her feet, still glancing toward the back door, apparently torn between staying with them and going after Randall.

Audrey dropped to her knees beside Beth and gathered her in her arms.

"Where's Mia?" Jackson asked.

"In the master bedroom closet. Go. Get her," Audrey urged him. "I have this."

He handed her the gun. "Shoot him if he so much as steps up to the door."

"Believe me, I will," she said, her voice steady. She let go of Beth and used both hands to point the gun at the broken back door.

Jackson hurried down the hallway and was back in less than a minute with the still-sleeping baby in his arms.

Audrey helped Beth to her feet and, together, she and Jackson guided them down the hallway to the nursery, where Beth tucked Mia into the baby crib, draping a soft, crocheted baby blanket around her. "If it's all right by you two, I'll sleep in here tonight."

"I wouldn't want it any other way," Audrey said. The twin bed in one corner had clean sheets and would keep Beth close to Mia through the night.

Jackson and Audrey backed out of the room and pulled the door closed halfway.

"Are you all right?" Jackson asked, staring at her face, his thumb brushing just below her throbbing cheekbone.

"I'm okay, just a little bruised and sore. I'll be all right with a dose of ibuprofen."

"Let me get that for you." He took her hand and led her into the kitchen and sat her at the kitchen table. His boots crunched across the broken glass as he made his way to the medicine cabinet for a couple pills, grabbed a glass from the dish drainer and filled it with water. Back across the broken glass, he handed her the items.

"Thank you." She took the pills and washed them down with the water, glad she could swallow after almost being choked to death.

Jackson stood beside her, a scowl marring his dark brows. "Maybe we should take you to the doctor."

"I'm fine. All I want to do is soak in a hot bath and sleep." When he started to protest, she held up her hand. "Really, Jackson. I'd tell you if I needed more than that. And I won't leave Beth and Mia here alone."

His frown remained for a few seconds longer and then he nodded. "Okay. But if you show any signs of internal injury or concussion, I'm calling an ambulance."

She smiled. "Deal."

"I'll board up the window in the back door and fix the front door before we go to bed," Jackson said, his face grim and pale for a swarthy-skinned Kiowa.

"Thanks, babe." Audrey leaned up and kissed his mouth, wincing when she realized her lip was split.

"When I get done shoring up the house, I'll come take care of that lip and bring you a bag of ice for your cheek." Jackson pressed a quick kiss to her forehead.

"I'll clean up the glass in the kitchen—" she started

to say.

"No." Jackson shook his head. "Go run a bath and soak. I won't be long."

Audrey let him go, too tired and achy to argue.

In the master bathroom, she turned the handles on the bath faucet, adjusted the temperature to warm, and poured in scented bath salts. The fragrant smells made her feel better. While the big tub filled, she returned to the bedroom and cleaned up the glass and rock on the floor. As tired and achy as she was, she took the time to vacuum to be certain all the glass shards were removed. She and Jackson liked padding barefoot and buck naked across the room. She didn't want that to change because a crazy man had violated their home.

When she was done with the vacuum, she left it in the hallway for Jackson to use in the kitchen.

Already she could hear the sound of a saw as Jackson fulfilled his promise to make the house safe again before they went to sleep.

Still a little shaky, Audrey retreated to the bathroom and slipped into the warm water, listening to the whirring buzz of a battery-operated drill gun.

Jackson would be screwing the board into the back door. Already she felt safer. He moved around to the master bedroom and screwed another board into the window frame.

Audrey sighed. For a short time, until they could replace the window, she wouldn't be able to enjoy the morning sun shining in to wake her.

She closed her eyes and leaned her head back on the edge of the tub, absorbing the heat into her sore muscles. She had a small bruise on her hip, her cheek-bone was puffy and her lip was split. She'd wiped away the blood with a bruised hand, the knuckles sore from being banged against the wall.

For a moment she considered wallowing in self-pity, but she reminded herself this was only a fraction of what Beth had put up with for the past six years.

Anger pushed aside self-pity. Beth would not go back to that man if Audrey and Jackson had anything to do with it.

A warm chuckle made her open her eyes, and she stared up at Jackson, unbuttoning his chambray shirt.

His lips twisted. "You look ready to spit nails. I would have thought a bath would relax you."

"I needed you in it with me."

"While you were daydreaming about clobbering bad guys, Cramer came back."

She sat forward. "Did they get him?"

"He said they'd set up a roadblock in both directions on the highway. They caught Randall Neal heading south toward Austin."

Audrey sat back in the water and let go of the breath she'd been holding. "Thank God. We might actually sleep tonight."

"Mind if I join you?" He dropped the shirt from his shoulders, and all those lovely muscles honed from hard ranch work rippled in the candlelight.

Audrey's core tensed, her pulse quickening. "You know I don't mind. Bring that naked body into this tub before I go crazy with lust. My pussy is on fire and there's only one way to quench it."

"I love it when you talk dirty to me." He flipped the button loose on his jeans, and his hand hesitated on the zipper. "I just want to make sure you got all your anger out on Randall. Cramer said Randall had a huge bruise on his forehead. I take it you gave it to him?"

"Damn right I did. If I had it to do all over, I'd have shot him dead and saved everyone time and money."

"This way, you won't go to jail on some stupid technicality." Jackson toed off his boots, unzipped and shoved the jeans off. For a moment he stood, naked and magnificent, his cock jutting out, straight and thick.

Audrey ran her tongue across her lip, anxious to feel that big, hard shaft thrusting inside her. She thanked her lucky stars she'd managed to snare this Kiowa cowboy for herself.

Then he slipped into the water beside her, making a wave that splashed up and over her and onto the tile floor. Gathering her in his arms, he sighed. "Ah. This is better."

She snuggled close, her hand stroking his thigh beneath the water. "Much better."

"I'd suggest we get it on..." his arms tightened gently, "...but seeing as how you're injured, I'm afraid to touch you."

"Every bone in my body would have to be broken to keep me from making love to you, Jackson Gray Wolf." She rolled over to straddle his hips, her knees on either side of him. "I could never get enough of you." She started to kiss him, but paused. "Unless, of course, my bruises are too painful for you to look at, and I'm too ugly to get laid."

He laughed. "Hardly. They're positive proof that you're the girl for me. You're not afraid of anything."

"Yes, I am." She pressed a kiss to his forehead and one to each of his cheeks. "I'm horribly afraid of losing you."

"Babe, you don't know the half of it. I lost five years off my life tonight." He shoved his hand through his hair, his face sober. "When I came back to the house, I knew something was wrong, and I couldn't get to you fast enough. I should never have gone."

"Yeah. Hindsight is always better than foreseeing the future. I should have known the fire at the Ugly Stick was a diversion. Randall may be crazy, but he's smart."

"I'm glad you're okay. I never would have forgiven myself if you'd been…if you…" He pulled her into his arms and buried his face against her neck. "I love you, Audrey. I can't imagine life without you."

"And I can't imagine life without you." She dug her fingers into his hair and tipped his face up so that she could claim his lips in a searing kiss, both passionate and desperate.

When she broke off the kiss, she pushed up on her knees and eased down over his member, taking him into her. "You make me complete," she said, her breath catching as he filled her so deliciously full.

He surged upward, pressing her thighs down, careful not to touch her bruised hip. "If it's me and you the rest of our lives, I'm perfectly happy. I love you."

With Jackson buried deep inside her, Audrey paused. "Jackson, if we can't make a baby of our own, what do you think about adopting one?"

"You want to talk about that now?" he asked.

Audrey shrugged. "It was just a thought. I could see adopting a baby like Mia or a child who doesn't have parents, or maybe the parents can't care for it."

His hands curled around her thighs. "I don't know, Audrey, I hadn't really thought about it. Who do you go to for something like that? Doesn't it take a long time and don't you have to jump through a lot of legal hoops? It always seemed a little cold and impersonal, like buying a puppy at a pet store. I love you, babe. I don't have to have a baby in the mix to improve our relationship. What we have together is enough for me." Jackson brushed her hair behind her ears. "Let me think about it."

Though her heart was heavy with disappointment over not having a baby of her own, Audrey agreed life was wonderful with Jackson in it. "It was just a thought." She rose and lowered herself over him again and again, moving faster and faster. Jackson's face grew tense and his hands tightened around her thighs. When she thought he might come, he stopped and lifted her off him, standing her on her feet.

"I wasn't done," she pouted.

He stood, water running off him in rivulets. "Neither was I." Stepping out of the tub, he helped her out and dried her off, his touch so gentle and caring, it made Audrey want to cry.

She toweled him off then, taking her time over his cock, cupping his balls and rolling them around in her fingers.

His chest expanded on a deeply indrawn breath, and

he captured her wrist in his hand. "Enough." Then he scooped her up in his arms and marched through the bathroom into the bedroom, where he tenderly laid her on the sheets.

For a moment he studied her bruises, his jaw hardening.

"Don't think about it." She reached out and cupped his ass, loving the feel of the hard muscles beneath his smooth skin. "Just love me."

"That was my plan." He spread her legs and lay down between them. Starting at the insides of her knees, he kissed a path up the sensitive skin of her inner thighs, angling ever closer to her heated core. When he reached her center, he tongued her entrance, swirling around the juices, suckling her nether lips until she was so turned on she could hardly remain still.

Audrey threaded her fingers in his thick black hair and dragged him farther up to the tuft of hair covering her most sensitive spot.

Jackson chuckled, his warm breath stirring her hairs. "Eager little thing, aren't you?"

"Damn right," she agreed through gritted teeth, her breath caught and held until he finally parted her folds and stroked her there.

Digging her heels into the mattress, she lifted her hips, positioning herself closer to his mouth, wanting more. "Please. Do it again."

"Your wish is my command." He licked a long, sensuous stroke along the length of that bundle of nerves, setting them off like firecrackers, bursting one after the other in rapid succession.

Audrey tipped her head back and moaned, the tension pulling tight as she neared the edge.

One more stroke and she launched into the stratosphere, tingling sensations erupting from her core outward, spreading to the very tips of her extremities. She rocked her pelvis, savoring every bit of her orgasm all the way up to the last shudder. When she fell back to earth, she dragged Jackson up her body, anxious to complete the magic with him coming inside her, hard, hot and wet.

But he wasn't in a hurry. Resisting her efforts to pull him onto her, he slowly worked his way up her torso, stopping to suck a beaded nipple into his mouth, rolling it around on his tongue and then nipping playfully.

"Ouch!" Audrey slapped his shoulder lightly.

"Does that hurt?" He backed away.

"Yes." She offered him the untouched one. "Please do the other the same way."

He laughed and complied, tonguing, nipping and flicking until she grabbed his buttocks and brought him the rest of the way home.

When he slipped inside her, she sighed. "I love it when you make love to me. It's magic from the moment you touch me to the moment we fall asleep in each other's arms."

"Sweetheart, if I'm making you sleepy, I'm not doing it right." Jackson thrust into her and withdrew all the way to the tip, teasing her.

Audrey raised her buttocks off the mattress, not wanting him to sever their connection. "Please, give me more."

He bent her knees and guided them up toward her ears. Then he feasted his gaze on that most intimate of connections where his shaft entered her. His eyes flashed and he held her legs as he pumped into her, his hips moving faster and faster.

Audrey lost track of the last breath she took, her body recovering from her previous orgasm in time to peak again on Jackson's final thrust.

He threw his head back and slammed into her, burying his cock until his balls bumped against her anus. Holding her thighs, he remained inside her for a full minute, his member throbbing against the walls of her channel.

She'd never felt more complete than when she made love to him.

When he released her legs, she wrapped them around his waist and drew him down to her, his cock still thick inside.

Jackson lay over Audrey, careful not to crush her. So gentle and caring.

Audrey loved this man more than she ever thought she could love one individual. Perhaps she was better off not getting pregnant. How could she possibly have enough room in her heart for anyone else? She sighed.

"I've never been happier," she whispered. "My life with you is perfect."

"And mine with you." Jackson kissed her and rolled to his side, taking her with him. "I wouldn't change a thing."

CHAPTER NINE

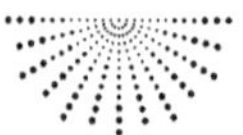

"Are you ready for us to open the doors?" Charli shouted across the bar to where Audrey stood beside the giant Christmas tree they'd erected on the edge of the dance floor, beside the stage.

Audrey took Jackson's hand and nodded. "Yes. Open them." She couldn't wait to show Jackson the gift she'd bought him.

Christmas Eve at the Ugly Stick Saloon was always a happy, lively occasion when everyone in the tri-county area seemed to congregate at the bar for the best Christmas Eve party in the state of Texas.

This Ugly Stick Christmas was even more special because Audrey had learned a valuable lesson over the past year. She learned that she was one of the luckiest women in the world to have Jackson in her life, and that she shouldn't get so caught up in wishes that she didn't see the blessings right in front of her.

Beth was working with Clayton Chance, and her

divorce would be final by the beginning of the new year. Her soon-to-be ex-husband was in jail on arson and aggravated assault charges. His career as an attorney and any aspirations toward political office were over, and if he got out of jail, he wasn't to come anywhere near Beth or Mia ever again.

Audrey had finally found the perfect gift for Jackson, and she could hardly wait for him to open the small package she'd placed beneath the tree.

Though she was happy, she hadn't been feeling on top of the weather for the past week. She assumed she'd gotten a case of food poisoning or a stomach bug because she couldn't keep food down and her stomach was always in a state of upset. With the most minor of smells, she'd be running toward the bathroom to toss her last meal.

Jackson had been busy with the ranch, with the delivery of a new colt and with helping the twins settle their new stallion in the barn. He'd also helped Beth move into a rental house in Temptation, where she and Mia would be closer to the stores and Mona, who'd insisted on babysitting in the evenings when Beth worked at the Ugly Stick. And Beth was going to school online during the day to become a nurse.

After having Beth and Mia in the house for almost three weeks, Audrey had fallen head over heels for the tiny Mia. Beth had asked her and Jackson to be Mia's godparents.

Once Beth had saved enough tips, she put a deposit and the first month's rent on a house in Temptation, a cozy little cottage with a white picket-fenced yard that would be perfect for Mia to play in.

Audrey hated to see them go, but knew Beth needed to learn how to be on her own. On moving day, she'd insisted on Beth taking the baby crib and dresser to furnish Mia's room in her new home.

Since she and Jackson had given up the idea of having a baby of their own, she saw no need in having a nursery. After the rush of Christmas and the New Year, she'd paint the walls a neutral color and turn the room back into a guest bedroom, erasing the sad reminder of their inability to have children. She assuaged her sadness with the thought that maybe someday Mark, Luke and Libby would grace them with nieces and nephews.

The bar filled quickly with all the people Audrey knew and loved. Many of them had found each other at the Ugly Stick and came to give thanks for the bar and the magic it seemed to bring them.

Lacey and Nick McBride arrived, carrying a large potted poinsettia.

Lacey set the plant on the stage, kissed Audrey on the cheek and Jackson on the lips and winked. "I didn't think Audrey would mind. She knows you love her." She wiped the lipstick off his lips and turned to a frowning Nick. "And I love you, babe. You should know that by now."

"Yeah, but I'd rather you saved your kisses for me." He pulled her tight against his side and captured her lips with a passionate kiss, bending her over his arm with a dash of cowboy drama.

When he brought her back upright, her eyes were glazed and her lips slightly swollen. She cupped his ass and ground her pelvis against his crotch. "Well. We said our hellos and Merry Christmases. Let's go back home to bed where you can make all my wishes come true."

Audrey laughed at Lacey's openly sexual advances. It was just like her to be so blatant. And the quiet cowboy she loved flushed a ruddy red.

Nick shook his head, a mischievous glint in his eyes. "I'm not ready to go. I want you good and hot before we head home." He grabbed her hand and swung her out on the dance floor into a buckle-rubbin' tight hold that left no room for air between them.

Kendall Mason and Ed Judson arrived, carrying a big wrapped box between them. Jackson hurried to take Kendall's end, and together the men laid the huge box beneath the tree.

Audrey shook her head. "What's with the giant present?"

Kendall gave her a secret smile. "It's a surprise."

"I hope it's not for me. I gave you extra bonuses to spend on yourselves, not me."

"It's a gift and it would be rude of you to refuse it, so hush," Kendall said with a stern glance at Audrey. "Now let me get to work or these people will start yammering for their alcohol."

"Jackson, Mark, Luke and I will be serving tonight. It's a party for all our friends and family. And you, Kendall and Ed, are family." Audrey hugged her. She'd watch the young woman blossom from an immature college co-ed to a wonderfully vibrant woman with Ed's love and attention. The man never knew what hit him when Kendall decided he was the man for her and set out to prove it to him.

Isabella, Gabe, Sean and Tanner O'Brien arrived, laughing and hugging each other as they joked about something that had happened on the drive over from the Rocking O Ranch. Their father Jonathon brought up the rear with his daughter Molly on his arm.

Audrey sucked in a deep breath, already tired though the evening had just begun. And she had so many people to serve. Yet she smiled and greeted the O'Briens with a warm welcome. "I'm so glad y'all could make it."

"We wouldn't miss it for the world." Isabella hugged Audrey. "It's been a wonderful year and we couldn't think of a better way to celebrate than with the people who mean the most to us."

"That's right." Gabe kissed Audrey's cheek. "If you hadn't had the good sense to hire Isabella, Sean, Tanner and I wouldn't have met her and we wouldn't be expecting a baby now."

Audrey's eyes rounded and she struggled for only a moment with the green-eyed monster of envy before letting it go. "I'm so very happy for you," she said, and meant it. "When is it due?"

"Late June." Isabella patted her still-flat tummy. "Hopefully before the summer gets too hot."

Audrey could tell by the color in her cheeks that Isabella was thrilled. "You are absolutely glowing."

She snorted softly. "I wasn't for the first two months. I couldn't eat, sleep, sit or stand without throwing up. Every little smell made me nauseous."

"Thank goodness she's past the morning sickness," Sean said.

Tanner laughed and patted Isabella's bottom. "Now she wants to eat *everything*."

Audrey laughed. "You're eating for two. Don't let anyone deprive you of that luxury."

"I'll gnaw their arms off if they try." Isabella winked and turned to her three men. "Who's going to ask me to dance first?"

Gabe, Sean and Tanner all answered as one. "Me!"

All four of them eased onto the dance floor, leaving Jonathon and Molly.

"What do you hear from Jesse and Ella?" Audrey asked Jonathon.

"They are staying in New York City over the holidays. Ella's show runs into the new year. Since she's the new kid on Broadway, she doesn't want to ruin her chances by taking time off. And she's saving up her favors to ask off when Isabella has her baby."

Audrey turned to Molly. "What about you? No date?" She glanced around the young woman as if searching for a hidden man.

Molly shrugged. "No date." She looked around the saloon. "Seems like I need to come to work at the Ugly Stick to fall in love. Every woman you've hired has found the cowboy of her dreams here."

"Say the word." Audrey smiled. "I'll put you to work."

Molly shook her head. "It's tempting but, no, thanks. I'm not in the market for a cowboy."

Jackson chuckled. "Just when you say you're not

looking or wishing, stuff happens." He hugged Audrey. "I wasn't really looking when I found Audrey."

Audrey snorted. "Oh, you were looking all right."

"Well, how could I not when you were stripping for me?" He kissed her and slapped her fanny. "Come on, we have guests to feed and keep liquored up."

"Audrey!" Lucky Albright entered with Trent and Isaac Moore on either one of her arms. She lifted her hand and waved, tripped over her own boots and nearly took Trent and Isaac down with her. Smiling awkwardly, she righted herself and hugged Audrey. "Thank you for inviting us to the party."

"Wouldn't have been a party without you."

"Hopefully I won't burn down the place." Lucky winked. "Oh wait, someone else beat me to that attempt."

"We'll try to hold off on the twisters while she's here," Trent teased.

"Lately, we keep the twists in the sheets." Isaac draped an arm over Lucky's shoulders and nodded toward the dance floor. "Wanna dance?"

Lucky sighed. "I have two left feet."

"Then they will match my two right feet just fine," Isaac said.

"Just a minute." Lucky held out a package to Audrey. "This is for you."

"Really? I'm feeling like I didn't come prepared. The invitation said no presents." Audrey accepted the gift. "But thank you." She set the package under the tree, shaking her head as Isaac and Trent led Lucky out onto the dance floor in a lively Cotton-Eyed Joe.

"Why are they all bringing gifts? I don't have anything to give them." Audrey leaned into Jackson, her eyes misting. She must be getting close to her time of the month. Lately she was getting overly emotional about everything.

Mona Daley and Grant Raleigh arrived carrying covered dishes and a brightly wrapped package.

"Hey Audrey, Jackson. I brought my mother's best spinach dip and some chicken wings. I wasn't sure what you'd have here, and I know my man loves to eat." Mona stepped up to her and waved the dip beneath her nose.

"Thank you, Mona—" The scent of sour cream and spinach wafted into Audrey's nostrils and turned her stomach inside out. She clapped a hand over her mouth and swayed.

"Are you feeling okay?" Grant frowned. "You're looking a bit pale."

Audrey fought the urge to purge and nodded, dropping her hand. "How are you since your accident, Grant?"

He stood straight. "Almost like new, except for the occasional twinge in my rib cage. The doc said I could go back to bull riding in a couple months, if I wanted to."

Mona was already shaking her head. "Over my dead body."

Grant grinned. "I know, sweetheart. I have better things to do staying right here with your live, and might I add, very pretty body." He nuzzled her neck and made her giggle.

"Oh sorry." Mona pulled free of Grant long enough

to hand the brightly wrapped package to Audrey. "This is for you."

"I have everything I need," Audrey protested. "And I didn't get anything for anyone."

Charli stepped up to her and slid an arm around her waist. "Audrey, you've given everyone so much. Let us do a little for you."

"Y'all are too nice."

"No. We love you and want you to be happy." Charli handed Audrey a mug of cider. "Here, you look like you could do with a drink."

Still leery of the stability of her stomach, Audrey accepted the drink and raised it to her lips. One sip of the cinnamon-and-apple-flavored liquid and her stomach rebelled. This time, there was no stopping it. She broke free of the people around her and ran for the bathroom, making it into a stall before the contents of her belly shot up her throat. After a few minutes, she stood and flushed the toilet, feeling remarkably more human.

"Better?" Charli stood outside the stall with a wad of wet paper towels in her hand. "Here, you might need to apply this to your face."

"That bad?" Audrey touched her cheeks.

"No, but it'll feel good."

"I don't know what's wrong with me. I must have caught a bug or something." Audrey frowned. "Maybe I should go home to keep anyone else from getting it."

"Oh, honey, I don't think any of us will get what you have."

Before Audrey could ask her what she meant, Charli

handed her a glass she'd pilfered from the bar. "Rinse your mouth and come back to the party. It won't be the same without you."

"If you're sure."

"I'm sure."

Charli held Audrey's hair back from her face while she splashed water over her cheeks and rinsed her mouth. When Audrey straightened, she said, "Thanks, Charli. You're a good friend."

"Damn right I am. And only a good friend would know when something's different."

Audrey tilted her head. "What do you mean?"

"You'll see. Now come on. We have a surprise for you."

Charli hooked Audrey's arm and led her back into the main bar.

Bunny, Cory and Jack had arrived and waved at her as she passed.

Charli refused to let her stop to say a proper hello, hauling her straight to the Christmas tree. Jackson stood there, a secret smile twitching around his lips.

Audrey's brows pushed together. "Am I the only one who doesn't know what's going on?"

Jackson nodded and winked.

Charli raised her fingers to her lips and blew a sharp, ear-splitting whistle, cutting through the chatter and laughter.

Everyone turned to face the Christmas tree and the three of them standing there.

Audrey's cheeks burned as all eyes focused on her

expectantly. "Thank you, Charli, but I really didn't have a big speech prepared."

Charli grinned. "That's okay. I do." She turned to the crowd. "As you all know, Audrey is like the grand dame for collecting strays—human strays, that is—in such a way that everyone who has come to work at the Ugly Stick Saloon has found their way back to a healthy, happy life. In the process of rebuilding our lives, we've found love and companionship that makes us that much richer and more complete."

"I'm not responsible for all that," Audrey protested.

Charli nodded. "Yes, you are. You have the biggest heart of anyone around here and have brought us together as a community. We all wanted to show our appreciation for you and just how much you mean to us. Thus the gifts."

Moving aside, Charli waved her hand toward the Christmas tree. "We know how much you want to have children, and perhaps one day soon, that will happen. But in the meantime, please accept our gifts. We give them with all the love in our hearts to a person who has shown us nothing but the love in hers."

Audrey's eyes welled with tears and she pressed a hand to her tightening chest. "Please," she started, afraid she'd lose it and start bawling in front of everyone. "Y'all are too nice. I don't deserve a bunch of gifts."

Charli held up a hand. "Wait, I'm not done. This gift is from all of us." She nodded to the side of the stage. "Bring it out."

Connor Mason and Ed Judson came out from behind

the curtains, carrying what appeared to be a long, rectangular item big enough to be a twin-sized mattress. It was covered in a black tarp. When they tore off the tarp, Audrey exclaimed, "Oh my God. It's beautiful!"

The men held a large sign with *Ugly Stick Saloon* written in neon lights. On one corner of the sign was a pair of red neon cowboy boots like the ones Audrey loved to wear. On the other end of the sign was a big red neon heart.

Audrey's knees wobbled and the tears trembled on her lashes, spilling over. "You shouldn't have. It had to have been horribly expensive."

"Don't cry, Audrey." Charli rushed forward. "We pooled our money and had it made especially for you."

Audrey smiled up at Jackson. "Oh, babe, I truly am blessed."

"Let them finish," he urged her.

Charli's lips twisted and then broke into a grin. "The sign was my idea."

Audrey hugged Charli. "It's perfect."

Bunny stepped forward with Cory and Jack, and took the gift she'd brought out from under the tree and handed it to her. "Careful, it has thorns." She laid it in Audrey's arms.

Audrey tore off the paper and stared down at what looked like a twig. She gave Bunny a confused look. "What is it?"

"A start from my grandmother's rosebush. Plant it in your garden and watch it grow along with all the love you and Jackson will share. Just like you've done with us, pay it forward to the next generation every chance you get."

Audrey's eyes rounded. "Is this a cutting from that huge red rosebush at the side of your shop?"

Bunny nodded. "I planted it from the start my mother gave to me from my grandmother's rosebush. Roots are important to a family."

"Thank you," Audrey said. "I'll cherish it."

Mona handed her a wrapped package and stood back. "Open mine."

Audrey smiled. "Y'all got me a sign. This is too much."

"Fine, I'll open it." Mona ripped the paper off and handed her the gift. It was a beautiful silver hairbrush with Audrey's initials engraved on the handle.

"I know," Mona said. "Who needs a silver hairbrush these days?" She shrugged. "No one, but a beautiful woman with a heart of gold deserves a little bling on her dresser. I love doing your hair, not because it's my job, but because you're a true friend and I can always count on you to have my back." Mona hugged Audrey. "I love you, girl. That brush comes with a free cut and style." She winked and stepped back.

Overwhelmed by the gifts, Audrey wiped tears from her eyes. "Before I open any more gifts and dissolve into tearful puddle, I want to give Jackson his present."

"I don't need anything but you, sweetheart. Besides, when did you have time to shop for me?" Jackson laughed and hugged her around the middle. "I love you."

Audrey dug the tiny box out from under the tree and handed it to him.

He opened it, revealing a key. "What's this?"

With a grin, Audrey waved toward the door. "Your present is in the parking lot outside. That key goes with it."

"What is it?" Jackson stared down at the key.

"Come outside and see." Audrey grabbed his hand and dragged him toward the front door and out into the parking lot.

A soft December breeze cooled Audrey's heated cheeks as she stood back and watched Jackson's reaction as, on cue, Nick McBride drove a bright red, vintage Corvette up in front of the saloon.

"This is the gift?" Jackson stood still, staring at the beautifully painted vehicle.

"Yes, silly." Audrey's brow furrowed. "Don't you like it? Mark and Luke said you had one growing up and missed it." She shot a confused look at her brothers-in-law.

Mark shrugged. "He said he always regretted trading it for the truck."

Audrey touched Jackson's shoulder. "If you don't like it, I can sell it and find something else."

"No, no. I love it." He turned toward her, not having taken one step closer to the car. "But it only has two seats."

Audrey nodded. "I know. It's a convertible sports car. They usually only have two seats."

He pulled an envelope out of his pocket and handed it to her. "As much as I like it, a two-seater doesn't really work with my gift to you."

Audrey took the envelope. "This is my gift?"

"They say big things can come in little packages," Charli said. "Open it."

The intense glance Jackson was giving her made her hand shake as Audrey lifted the flap and extracted what appeared to be a brochure.

When she held it up to the light, she could read the name of a company specializing in…adoptions.

Her heart squeezing hard in her chest, Audrey looked up into Jackson's eyes. "Are you sure?"

He smiled, pulling her into his arms. "Never more certain. You will make a wonderful mother to a child, so how could I deprive a child of the opportunity to have you for its mother? And I promise to be a good father and love it as much as you do."

If her heart could swell any bigger, Audrey's would have exploded out of her chest, she was so happy. "Thank you. This is the best gift ever." She wrapped her arms around him and hugged him for a long time.

"A-hem." Charli cleared her throat beside Audrey. "We have something to say as well."

Audrey shook her head. "I'm so happy, I can't possibly accept any more gifts."

"Well, to add to Jackson's hugely awesome gift, we want you to know we'll help you do what it takes and even vouch for you if you choose to adopt."

Audrey reached out and hugged Charli. "This is too much. I would never ask you to do that for us."

"We know you wouldn't ask, but we all want to help." Charli nodded toward the crowd. "Show of hands who would volunteer?"

Libby, Beth, Kendall, Lacey, Bunny, Mona, Isabella

and Lucky all raised their hands, followed by all the men in the bar.

Charli faced Audrey. "You see, we love you and want you to be happy. You'll make a wonderful mother."

Audrey smiled through her tears. If not for Jackson's arm around her, she would have sunk to the floor, she felt so loved. "Thank you all. I have the best family a woman could hope for. All of you!" She glanced up through her tears, her stomach picking that moment to turn upside down. "Please, everyone, let's go back inside and enjoy the party."

She entered the saloon and held on until the music started and the crowd of friends and family hit the dance floor before she said to Jackson, "Excuse me." Then she ran to the bathroom, where she lost what little was left in her belly.

Jackson came in behind her and held her hair while she pulled herself together.

"I don't know what's wrong with me," she said weakly.

"If I didn't know better, I'd say you were experiencing morning sickness."

Audrey froze. How long had it been since her last cycle? With all that had happened with Beth and Mia and preparing for the Christmas party, she'd forgotten to keep track. "What day is it?" she asked.

Jackson chuckled. "Christmas Eve, babe. Remember? The party?"

Audrey clapped a hand to her forehead. "Could you have Charli get my purse for me?"

Jackson frowned. "Why?"

"Just do it," she urged. "Please."

Jackson left the bathroom and returned carrying her purse. "Is there something I can do for you?"

"Yes." She dug in her purse for the box she'd been carrying since the last time she'd ovulated, as the power of positive thinking. It was still there. "You can pray." She took the purse into the stall, dug out the pregnancy test, removed the packaging, dropped her pants and peed.

"Are you doing what I think you're doing?" Jackson asked.

"If you mean am I taking a pregnancy test?" Audrey called out through the door a she held the wand in position. "Then yes." She straightened and pulled her jeans up with one hand.

The door opened and Jackson stood there. "Well?"

She held the wand up. "We have to give it time to process."

"No we don't." Jackson stared at the screen on the wand.

"What do you mean, no we don't?" Audrey jerked her hand back and read the display, prepared for the usual disappointment. In the screen was the single word.

Pregnant.

"Holy hell, Audrey, you're pregnant!" Jackson picked her up and spun her around. "We're going to have a baby!"

Still too gun-shy to believe it, Audrey waited until Jackson set her on her feet. When he did, she stared at the stick again. The word *Not* never appeared.

Her heart filled and her chest swelled. "Sweet Jesus. I didn't think life could get any better than it already was."

Jackson kissed her and held her close. "Babe, wishes really can come true."

Audrey couldn't stop smiling. Yes, indeed, wishes really could come true. She was pregnant and tomorrow was Christmas.

"I know something that could make life even better." Jackson's eyes took on a devilish gleam. "That is, if you're feeling okay."

Audrey stood straight, feeling better than she had in days. "I'm feeling wonderful. What did you have in mind?"

He grabbed her hand and led her into the costume room behind the stage, where Audrey kept the props for the once-a-month strip shows the Ugly Stick Saloon was famous for. He pulled a pair of chaps off a hanger and handed them to her, then pulled another pair out and grabbed a black leather riding crop.

Audrey's stomach fluttered in a good way as she led him behind a stage prop. As soon as they were well hidden from sight of any staff member passing by, she pulled off her boots so that she could get her jeans off. Then she put her boots back on, shed her shirt and tied on the chaps. Wearing a lacy black bra and matching black lace, thong panties, she grabbed the crop and faced her man, her heart thumping hard against her ribs.

He had taken off everything and now stood before her in nothing but his boots and the chaps. His cock jutted out straight and hard. A frown dented his brow and he asked, "Making love won't hurt the baby, will it?"

"No. If anything it will let the baby know how much his mommy and daddy love him."

"Good, because I couldn't possibly last nine months without making love to my beautiful wife." He held out his hand and winked. "I'll take that crop."

Audrey lifted her chin and ran the riding crop up the side of his leg. "Are you sure you can handle it?"

Jackson pulled her into his arms, his cock nudging her bare belly. "Babe, I'm only sure of one thing. And that's my love for you." He hooked a finger in her panties and dragged them down her leg in a long, sensuous glide, skimming her inner thigh with his fingers.

By the time Jackson pulled the panties over her red boots, Audrey was quivering, her nerves on fire and her pussy damp. "Oh, cowboy, I'm ready to ride."

Jackson lifted her and sat her on the closest box and stepped between her legs, his cock poised at her entrance. "One more thing."

Audrey moaned, so ready to have him inside her, fucking her like there was no tomorrow. "What?" She reached for his hips, determined to make it happen.

"Just thought you'd like to know, I found your missing box of whiskey."

She frowned, barely able to concentrate on his words. "Where?"

He laughed. "You're sitting on it." Without waiting for her response, he slid into her, his member filling her. She'd loved this man more than anything, and now she was going to have his baby.

She glanced down at where they were so intimately connected and prayed they would always be together and making love like teenagers in the prop room.

And damned if he wasn't right. The box she was sitting on had the words Jack Daniels Whiskey written in bold letters.

She laughed out loud, swallowing her mirth as Jackson thrust into her again and again, taking her to the stars in the heavens.

***If you enjoyed this book, try the other books in the
Ugly Stick Saloon Series***

Boots & Chaps (#1)
Boots & Sex Ed (#2)
Boots & Leather (#3)
Boots & Promises (#4)
Boots & Bareback (#5)
Boots & Dirty Tricks (#6)
Boots & Lace (#7)
Boots & Roses (#8)
Boots & Buckles (#9)
Boots & the Wishes (#10)
Boots & Twisters (#11)
Boots & the Bachelor (#12)
Boots & The Rogue (#13)
Boots & The Heartbreaker (#14)
Boots & Wings (#15)

BOOTS & TWISTERS

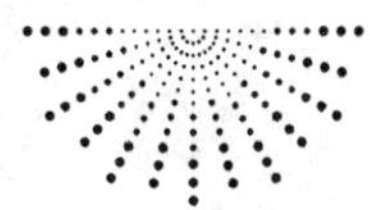

UGLY STICK SALOON SERIES BOOK #11

by Elle James
New York Times Bestselling Author

writing as

Myla Jackson

BOOTS & TWISTERS

UGLY STICK SALOON

New York Times Bestselling Author

ELLE JAMES

writing as

MYLA JACKSON

*L*ucky Albright had been driving all day and she still wasn't out of Texas. Worse, she had no idea where she was. With her gas gauge on empty, her stomach gnawing a hole clean through to her backside, and her wallet bone dry of remedying either of her first two issues, she pulled into the parking lot of the only building she'd seen since the last small town of Hole in the Wall. Maybe, just maybe, someone inside could point her to the nearest homeless shelter.

Because that was what she was.

Homeless.

She reached up to swipe at the ready tears, cursing herself for shedding even one when the people of Comfort, Texas, had been anything but a comfort to her. Hell, they'd run her out of town like an unwanted stray dog. All she'd been looking for was a quiet place to call her home. And they'd kicked her out after a series of unfortunate events that hadn't been her fault at all.

She could still picture the mayor of Comfort along with over half the town loading her meager belongings into her truck.

"Get out of town and stay out of town," the mayor had said. "In fact, get the hell out of Texas. Your kind is not wanted anywhere near the great Lone Star State."

Her kind?

With townsfolk lined up along the street, blocking her return to city limits, she had felt like she was part of a cartoon or a reality show about being punked. Surely this wasn't happening to her. She had every right to be in that town. Never in her life had she committed a crime, she followed rules, she was an upstanding citizen.

So she'd had a run of bad luck. It wasn't her fault Mitsy Grumbal's dog tangled with a skunk, Joe Sarli wrecked into the side of one of their precious historic buildings, Raymond Rausch's cow had gotten loose and trampled the flowers around the town square, or the public library had burned down. But somehow, she'd been the one closest to the incidents and she'd taken the blame. Taken wasn't exactly the term she'd use. Assigned was closer to reality.

As she drove through the parking lot packed with a Saturday night crowd, the tears blurred her eyes, but she refused to shed even one more. Before she could find a place to pull in, her engine sputtered and died. Her beat-up pickup drifted to a stop behind four large, shiny new trucks.

Empty.

Lucky leaned her head on the steering wheel,

fighting back more tears. "Fuck this!" she yelled, slamming her palm against the dash. "I'm an Albright. Albrights don't give up and they sure as shootin' don't cry." She unbuckled her seat belt, climbed down from the truck, tucked her hair up into her cowboy hat and strode for the front door of the building, glancing up at the crooked sign hanging overhead.

Ugly Stick Saloon.

Figured. She could use a beer about now, but she didn't have the money to buy one, much less a gallon of gas to get her into the next town. All she could hope for was to find work washing dishes, scrubbing toilets or, if her luck changed, landing a job with a rancher who needed a ranch hand. One who would give her a lift to the ranch until she could afford to put gas in her truck and bring it with her.

Music pulsed through the corrugated tin walls of the building. As Lucky stepped through the front entrance, she could hear the excited screams of the women inside.

A large gender-ambiguous person stood guard just inside the door, blocking her entrance. "Sorry, mister, it's Ladies Night. No men allowed."

Lucky didn't mind when people mistook her for a man. She was taller than most women and slender, more athletic than curvy. And she liked to wear men's jeans, chambray shirts and cowboy boots. The horses and cows she preferred to work with didn't care what she wore or how she wore it.

But right at that moment, she needed to get inside and find help. Either that or stay the night in her truck, blocking the four larger trucks in their parking spaces.

"Suits me just fine." She swept off the cowboy hat and let her long sandy-blond hair fall down about her shoulders. That too would have been cut short, but she hadn't had time or the spare cash to get it cut in the past couple months and it grew like hay in a warm summer rain.

The bouncer's eyes narrowed and gave her a swift appraising once-over before nodding. "There's a five-dollar cover charge to get in tonight." A meaty hand came out, palm up.

Crap. If she'd had five bucks, she wouldn't be out of gas at this point. She'd have bought a gallon in Hole in the Wall instead of risking another fifteen miles to Temptation. "Look, my truck...stalled out in the parking lot. I need to speak with the owner."

"Sorry, Audrey Anderson is busy."

Feeling more desperate by the second, Lucky put on her best poker face and insisted, "I need to speak with Ms. Anderson."

The bouncer crossed beefy arms over a broad chest. "Unless you pay the cover charge, you ain't gettin' in."

Defeated, Lucky trudged back to her truck. She couldn't leave it in the middle of the parking lot, blocking other vehicles from getting out. She put it in neutral and, rounded to the back and leaned with all her might against the tailgate. The heavy vehicle barely moved an inch.

Throwing all the anger and frustration she'd lived with over the past two years into her next push, she got the truck rolling. Grunting and pushing, she plowed her feet into the gravel and the vehicle moved faster.

Until that moment, Lucky hadn't noticed the slight slope leading to the far end of the parking lot, the line of trucks and the drainage ditch beyond.

Once the truck was in motion, she glanced up and froze momentarily.

The truck was now rolling at a good clip and headed straight for a bright red pickup, with a shiny paint job and a license plate that read USS1.

Lucky dug her heels into the gravel and leaned back, holding on to the bumper, but it did little slow the momentum, her worn boot heels kicking up lines of dust behind her.

"No," she said out loud, visions of the charred remains of the Comfort Public Library flooding her head. "Not again." She willed the strength of a bulldozer into her back and tried again to slow the vehicle.

It rolled faster, until it slammed into the back of the pretty red truck, forcing its front wheels over the edge of the embankment, where it teetered for a moment. Gravity and the weight of Lucky's truck gave it an added *oomph*, and it slid down into the drainage ditch below.

Her own truck followed the red truck into the ditch, metal crunching metal.

Catching herself before she too pitched over the edge, Lucky teetered on the embankment, staring down at the wreckage, her heart sinking into her boots.

"Holy shit."

Why was it when she thought things were really bad they got worse? The phrase *it only goes up from here* never entered her realm of possibilities.

She stood for a long time, staring at the trucks in the ditch, wondering how she'd talk her way out of this one.

"Fuck, Audrey's gonna be pissed," a voice said beside her. A pretty blonde stood with glazed eyes and a tight skirt just behind Lucky, swaying slightly.

"Yup. Audrey loves that truck. Almost as much as she loves her red boots," an equally pretty brunette said.

"I didn't mean for it to happen. It was an accident."

"Mister, you got some 'splainin' to do." The blonde hiccupped, pressed a hand to her lips and stared at the brunette, her eyes rounded and dancing with amusement.

The brunette with the big brown eyes giggled. "Shh. Mona, you're swayin'."

Mona hiccupped and pointed at the brunette. "Don't think you're so cool, Bunny. You're swayin' too."

They hugged each other, falling to the ground giggling.

Lucky's gut twisted. "Please tell me that truck didn't belong to Audrey Anderson, the owner of the Ugly Stick Saloon."

The women giggled more, rolling on the ground, Mona aware enough to say, "Okay, we won't tell you. Shh, Bunny, it's a secret."

"Fuck secrets." Bunny laughed again, her eyes filling with tears of senseless, uncontrollable mirth. "Jackson just bought her that truck to match her favorite boots."

"Do you suppose you could go back into the Ugly Stick Saloon and ask her to come outside?" Lucky asked, biting back her frustration at the two women's staggering inebriation.

"Sure," Mona said. "Wanna see her face when she realizes that's her truck in the ditch."

"Me too. Wait, where's *my* truck?" Bunny asked.

"You rode with me, silly. Besides, you don't own a truck."

"That's right." Bunny giggled.

"Do you two mind getting Audrey?" Lucky reminded them.

"Going," Mona responded. "Come on. Maybe we can see Cory dance again."

Lucky followed the two ladies to the door.

"Greta Sue, we're back," Mona sang and showed the bouncer the ink stamp on her wrist.

Bunny did the same and the bouncer allowed them inside, while Lucky received an eat-shit-and-die-because-you're-not-getting-inside-without-the-requisite-cover-charge look.

Greta Sue. Hell, who knew she was female?

Lucky held her breath as Greta Sue pointed at her, her gaze narrowing, warning her not to make any sudden moves.

Lucky waited, the acids in her empty stomach churning, eating a hole through the lining. What would she say to the owner of the Ugly Stick? Would she be like her bouncer, large, bulky and friggin' scary? Would she slam her into the ground with one thick stump of a fist and leave her there to die?

She'd considered death as an alternative, but Lucky had one problem with that…she liked living.

The scent of beer and grilled burgers drifted toward her from inside the bar and she swayed with hunger, not having eaten since the night before. She truly was in hell.

Greta Sue closed the door to the stomach-churning smells, leaving Lucky out in the dark. A minute passed, then two. Had the two ladies forgotten? As plastered as they were, that could have been the case.

Seven minutes passed before Lucky came to the sad conclusion the ladies had either gotten lost in the crowd, or forgotten. From all the whooping and hollering going on inside, Lucky guessed it was the latter.

She wondered if there was a rear entrance. If she could at least sneak inside and find Audrey, she could break the bad news and hopefully avoid going to jail. She rounded the tin building that vibrated with the sound of the sexy music and screams from the crowd. A door at the back opened and a woman stepped out carrying a bag of trash. She propped the door to keep it from shutting, then set off for the large trash bin set away from the building.

Her heart hammering, Lucky saw her break and took it. She ran for the door, careful not to make too much noise and ducked inside. The back of the building had a hallway with a room off to the left and another to the right. Footsteps on the porch behind her made her turn left. Her back to the room, she peeked out into the hallway, waiting for the person to pass by.

"Hey, buddy, you dancin' tonight?" a male voice said behind her. "Or are you lookin' for the poker game?"

Lucky spun, her cheeks burning and her jaw dropped. A truly beautiful man with long blond hair stood in front of her, wearing nothing but a G-string and chaps. He stuck out his hand. "Cory McBride."

"Lucky Albright," she said automatically.

"Nice to meet you. So what is it? Poker or dance?" He waved toward the other men in various states of undress. All equally as handsome as the man in front of her. Holy hell, they were strippers!

Lucky swallowed hard to ease her dry throat. "Poker," she eked out.

"Across the hall." Cory opened the door and pointed at another door.

"Thanks," she said.

"Don't you let them eat you alive."

Lucky glanced down the hallway. The coast was clear and she stepped out. When the door didn't close behind her, she glanced back at the man.

He nodded. "That's the one. Go on in."

It was go in or admit she wasn't there for either dancing or poker.

She chose the door to the right and walked in, turning to close it behind her.

A light glowed from around an inside corner.

"That you, Audrey?" a voice called out.

Lucky didn't answer, praying they'd think the door opened and closed and no one had actually entered.

"Guess it wasn't Audrey," the voice said. "I'm going for a refill on our pitcher of beer. Anyone have an objection to Budweiser? Jackson, Nick, Isaac?"

"Bring me back one of those horny women," one man called out. "And while you're at it get one for yourself. You've been too uptight lately. You really need a wife."

The others chuckled.

The voice moving nearer responded with, "I'm not ready to be shackled to someone who doesn't know a horse shoe from a stiletto."

"What you need is a good old-fashioned cowgirl. Boots, jeans, hat and all. No nonsense, no frills."

"That's exactly what I need, Jackson," the voice said.

"One who can ride a horse, drive a tractor and stay up all night with a sick cow," the one called Jackson added.

"You don't need a wife, you need a ranch hand."

"Nick, that's all well and good, but what would he do for sex?" Jackson asked.

The voice moving closer responded, "I can get that in the next county. There's a widow there who's more than happy to accommodate. No commitment required."

"Ah, that gets old."

"Hasn't yet."

"We should fix him up with someone local," Nick said.

"Got any ideas?" Jackson asked.

"The man's been picky all his life. Hasn't dated the same woman more than twice."

"All I ask is a woman who's faithful, doesn't nag, loves me and all my faults and doesn't care if I track mud on the floor." The voice sounded right next to Lucky.

One of the men chortled. "You just described my dog."

Lucky agreed, the man needed a dog, not a woman.

The man headed her way snorted. "Am I askin' too much?"

Yes. She bet he wasn't all that perfect, yet he was expecting perfection in a woman. *Jerk.*

"Yeah, big brother. When you find one like that, let me know."

"Hell, if you're nice to me, I might even share her with you. After all, what are brothers for?"

"Share, hell! I might arm wrestle you for her."

The man thought he could share a woman with his brother? What kind of asshole was he? It was as if the woman would have no say in the matter. No wonder he wasn't married. With his attitude, what woman would have him?

"Since I'm not likely to find one out in the crowd tonight, don't worry. You won't get your ass kicked at the arm wrestling."

"I hope your arm wrestling is better than your poker skills."

The men laughed while Lucky glanced around, looking for a place to hide and finding none. She whipped off her hat, letting her hair fall down around her shoulders. Surely the man wouldn't be threatened by a girl and throw a punch at her.

When the man rounded the corner, he stopped short, all his six-foot something, broad-shouldered, dark-haired gorgeousness. "What the hell?"

"You say something, Trent?" Jackson's deep voice called out.

Lucky pleaded with her eyes, pressing a finger to her lips. Holy hell, the man in front of her should have been on the other side of the hallway preparing to strip. He certainly had the body for it. And with his ego the size of Texas, he could pull it off.

Trent's eyes narrowed and he hesitated before replying, "No, just stubbed my toe." His gaze traveled the length of her.

"There's a light switch on the wall by the door," Isaac said.

"I'm okay, just a little unlucky. However, I have high hopes of getting luckier." His mouth curved upward in a smooth, sexy grin.

Lucky's heart beat faster and her knees wobbled. If she thought he was good looking before the smile… wow. And she usually didn't get all weak-kneed around men, seeing them as competition, not the prize.

"*We* hope your lousy luck holds true through the rest of the hands."

A rumble of chuckles sounded from the men out of sight.

Trent motioned toward the door with the empty plastic pitcher in his hand.

Lucky opened it slowly, peeked out and sighed when she'd determined that the door across the hallway was closed and the hallway itself was empty. She stepped out and turned around to face Trent so fast she knocked the pitcher from his hand. It skidded across the floor to the other side.

They both bent to pick it up at the same time.

Lucky reached it first, grabbed and jerked upright, her skull colliding with his nose.

"Damn!" Trent exclaimed.

Lucky's head smarted and she swayed at the pain. When she could focus her gaze on him, her heart sank to her wobbly knees.

Trent clutched his nose, his eyes watering, blood trickling down his chin.

"Oh hell. Did I do that?" Her belly clenched. If she could find a way to screw things up, she did. With a frantic glance around the empty hallway, she despaired of finding a towel to stem the flow of blood. With a desperate jerk, she pulled her shirt off her back, thankful she'd worn a tank top beneath the chambray. She held the garment up to his face. "Move your hands," she commanded.

He did, the blood dripping onto her shirt. She pressed the fabric to his nose gently. "I'm sorry. I didn't mean to hurt you. Are you okay?" she asked, staring into the most beautiful dark chocolate eyes she'd ever seen. She could fall right into those and get lost forever. Good grief! She'd never been this mesmerized by a man before. Ever.

Her pulse hammering against her ears, she pulled the shirt away from his nose. "It's already stopped bleeding."

"Good." He flung the shirt to the side, grabbed both of her wrists and pinned them to the wall above her head. "Perhaps you could tell me why you were hiding in the poker room, and why you were back here where only employees are allowed. I don't think I've seen you working here before." He pinned her body to the wall with his, not giving her room to raise her knee fast and hard enough to hit him where it counted.

She squirmed, fighting against his strong hold, the heat of his body against hers doing funny things to her insides. It had been a long time since a man had bested her and it infuriated her as well as sparked something in her that she'd thought long dead.

Lust.

And damned if he didn't smell good. Like saddle leather and a subtle aftershave. She loved the smell of leather and aftershave. It made her feel all girlie. With a gasp, she fought harder. "Let go of me. I was looking for Audrey Anderson."

"If you're here to rob her, you'll have to go through everyone else in the place to get to her." His grip tightened.

"I'm not here to rob Audrey or anyone else."

"Then what do you want with her?"

"None of your business."

"You made it my business when you snuck into our poker game."

Lucky chewed on her lip, hating that he held her so securely and hating even more that *her* body was reacting to *his* leaning against hers. "I have something to tell her."

"Tell me and I'll pass it on to her."

She straightened, her lips pressing into a tight line. She didn't like being manhandled—even if he smelled good enough to lick—and worse, she didn't want to confess her crime to this man. "I'll tell her what I came to say when I see her."

"Tell you what…I'll let the bouncer decide."

Lucky's eyes widened. As much as she disliked being detained by this man, the bouncer was a thousand times scarier. "I need to see Audrey. It's very important. And the bouncer wouldn't let me."

"Greta Sue won't let you? Why?"

"Because…" She searched for a good reason other than the truth. Shame made her cheeks burn. She didn't want to admit she was broke and couldn't afford the cover charge to get in. "Because. Damn it!"

"Not good enough."

Anger, shame, desperation roiled up and exploded. "I couldn't pay the cover charge to get in the front door. There! Are you satisfied?" Her bottom lip trembled and she bit into it to keep it steady. She'd never been down and out before in her life and it galled her no end. "Look, just let me talk to her and I'll leave as soon as I can." She'd have to walk, but she'd leave just to get away from the man and the way he made her heart pound like horses hooves on hard-packed dirt in an all-out gallop.

"Look, I'm feeling generous tonight. I'll get you that meeting with Audrey."

Hope surged, along with the dread of having to tell the owner of the bar she'd run her truck into a ditch. "You will?"

He nodded. "On one condition."

Her brows narrowed. She knew it was too good to be true. People always wanted something. Nothing ever came for free, and normally she was just fine with that, except now. She was broke. "What condition?"

"One kiss." His gaze shifted to her lips.

She struggled against his hold on her hands. "No."

He let go of one hand and dragged her toward the rear exit with the other.

She dug in her boot heels but got no traction from the smooth wood floors. He out-weighed her, out-muscled her and she could do nothing to stop him. Stubborn resignation set in. What good did it do to fight? He refused to relent and she was going nowhere. Lucky quit fighting and followed.

He opened the door and waved a hand toward the back parking area. "I suggest you take it up with Greta Sue at the front entrance."

Lucky assumed that because she hadn't fought him the last few steps, he thought she'd go willingly. When he let go of her hand, she let her shoulders sag as if defeated, but she was far from it.

"You're missing your chance to meet Audrey." His brows rose invitingly. "It won't cost you much. Just one little kiss."

Her chin tipped up. "When I kiss a man, it's because I want to, not because I need a favor. And frankly, I find nothing kissable about you." Her gaze traveled his length from tip to toe and heat flared, belying her words. There were far too many kissable things about this man, except for his inflated ego and his unrealistic views on a perfect woman. "Now, if you'll excuse me."

He stepped back to let her pass.

She stuck out her hand, offering to shake his.

Hoping he'd take it so that she could use the one trick she knew to subdue a randy cowboy. When he set his hand in hers, she twisted and yanked his hand up behind his back and between his shoulder blades, then planted her boot on his cute ass and shoved him through the doorway, slamming it shut behind him.

She spun so fast she almost fell. Then she ran in the opposite direction, hoping to get lost in the crowd before tall, dark and arrogant could catch up with her. Then maybe she'd find Audrey and break the bad news to her.

The door behind her slammed open, but she didn't turn to see who was there, knowing she only had seconds to make good her escape.

Coming from behind the bar, Lucky spied the bartender, a pretty woman with auburn hair, wearing black leather like she meant it.

"Excuse me," Lucky shouted over the rabid crowd of screaming women.

A man danced on the stage. One with long blond hair and a killer body dressed in nothing but a G-string.

Lucky recognized him as the man she'd met in the back. Cory, he'd said was his name. His body was perfect, one she'd love to stay and watch, if only she wasn't facing a huge bill to have the owner's truck fixed with money she didn't have. How did she manage to get in situations like this?

The bartender slapped five mugs of beer onto a tray before she turned to Lucky. "What can I get you?" she asked.

"Audrey Anderson?"

The bartender nodded toward the stage where a woman introduced the blond-haired man to the audience as Cory McBride. "She's the emcee, right now."

Lucky groaned. To get to her, she had to wade through tightly packed women who appeared to have staked their claims on their own pieces of the floor, unwilling to let anyone else get closer. They fought to place bills in the man's G-string and get their opportunity to grope.

Lucky snorted. This was not the scene for her. She wanted a man who didn't have to dance for a living. One who worked with animals. Feeling more comfortable around animals than people, Lucky was far out of her element in the packed barroom. But it couldn't be helped. She had to get to Audrey and let her know what had happened.

Trying not to step on anyone, she pushed her way through the crowd, taking elbows to the gut, her boots stomped on by other cowboy boots and some stilettos. All the while she kept a watch out for the bouncer.

The tighter the bodies pushed up against her, the shallower her breathing became. She'd never been good in tight places. Claustrophobia, her daddy had called it. Her heart pattered against her ribs, and her palms sweat. A moment before Lucky would have passed out, the pretty strawberry blonde wearing a pair of short shorts and red cowboy boots stepped down from the stage.

"Are you all right?" she asked, touching Lucky's arm.

Her vision graying around the edges, Lucky swayed

and didn't see the bouncer until she grabbed her from behind. "How'd you get in here?" she demanded.

"Greta Sue," the bar owner said. "She's not well. Let's get her out of this crush."

"I'll get her out. All the way out of the building. Plenty of air to breathe outside. She didn't pay the cover charge."

The strawberry blonde smiled. "It's okay. I'll cover for her this time."

"But, Ms. Anderson, she snuck in somehow. That's trespassin'."

"It's okay. I'm sure she has a good reason." Ms. Anderson led her to the edge of the jostling crowd and already Lucky could breathe better.

Lucky held her breath as Greta Sue pointed at her, her gaze narrowing, warning her not to make any sudden moves.

The strawberry blonde smiled and held out a hand to Lucky. "I'm Audrey Anderson, owner of the Ugly Stick Saloon. How may I help you?"

Her voice was warm, friendly and so likable it made Lucky want the floor to swallow her whole. Why couldn't Audrey Anderson have been old, ugly and mean-spirited? Breaking the bad news to this sweet woman made her feel even more of a heel.

Lucky took her hand and shook it, cringing inwardly, at a loss as to how to explain how she'd managed to wreck both her own truck and that of the pretty woman standing in front of her with the friendly smile and the firm handshake.

She cleared her throat and blurted, "I have some bad news."

Audrey's brows knit and she stepped closer. "Jackson. Is he all right?"

Lucky frowned. "Who's Jackson?"

"My boyfriend. I assumed the bad news was about him. Are you telling me it's not?"

With a shake of her head, Lucky waved her hand toward the doorway. "It's best I show you."

Greta Sue gave Lucky the stink-eye. "You hurt one hair on Ms. Anderson's head..." Audrey Anderson had her share of folks looking out for her. A stab of longing tugged at Lucky's heart. It would be nice to be loved that much by so many people.

Lucky raised her hands in surrender. "I'm not going to hurt her."

"Damn right you're not." Greta Sue followed them out the door. "I'm coming with you."

Great. More witnesses to Lucky's destruction and mortification.

"Tell me what happened." Audrey walked beside Lucky, her feet moving briskly in the night air, her bright red cowboy boots crunching gravel.

"I stalled out in the parking lot and didn't have any help moving my truck, so I pushed it. And well..." Lucky stopped where Audrey's red truck used to be parked.

The strawberry blonde's brows dipped together. Her gaze moved from the empty spot to glance around the parking lot. "Didn't I park my truck here? For that matter, I don't see it anywhere."

Lucky bit down on her lower lip, touched the Ugly Stick owner's arm and pointed to the ditch. "It's in there."

Audrey stepped up to the edge of the embankment and stared down at the shapes of the two trucks wedged into the ditch at angles. As recognition dawned, she gasped. "That's my new truck!"

TRENT COULDN'T BELIEVE a girl had bested him. Isaac, Nick and Jackson would all have laughed had they witnessed his humiliation. Strange that the embarrassment and fact that he'd been tricked only made him that much more determined to get that kiss.

No sooner had he been shoved out the door, he turned, caught the door before it closed and stormed back inside, only to see the tall, slender, cool drink of cowgirl water slip into the darkness of the bar. Well, hell. It was Ladies Night and Audrey had given them strict instructions to limit their movements to the employee-only area of the bar or risk being pinched, kissed, squeezed and fondled by a couple hundred horny women.

Trent debated following her, but he'd heard of how Jackson had been stripped to his skivvies once on Ladies Night and he had no desire to be exposed in such a way.

So he didn't get his kiss. What harm could one more woman add to a room full of raging estrogen?

He returned to the poker game and settled in, his mind on the cowgirl, not his hand. No sooner had

Jackson dealt the cards, Nick got a call to tow two trucks.

"Audrey, is that you?" Nick asked.

Jackson frowned. "Trouble?"

"Two trucks in the ditch out front." Nick tossed his cards on the table and rose. "I'll be right there."

"Two trucks?" Trent's brother, Isaac, asked. "Things must be hoppin' on Ladies Night."

"What's going on? The strippers try to make a run for it?" Trent joked, wondering if the woman he'd let go into the bar had anything to do with the trucks in the ditch. A jab of guilt twisted in his belly. He should have let Audrey know she'd had a trespasser.

"Sorry, guys," Nick said. "You're welcome to stay and play, but I've got work to do. Seems Audrey's was one of the trucks that got knocked into the ditch."

"Audrey's?" Jackson jumped to his feet. "She wasn't in it, was she?" Jackson checked his cell phone. "Fuck. I had my ringer off. Audrey's been tryin' to get a hold of me. She called three times." He punched the screen on his phone and held it to his ear.

"No, someone else's vehicle pushed it into the ditch. Come on. Let's check it out. I could use a hand getting them out."

"Maybe we should all go check it out." Trent tossed his hand onto the table and pushed to his feet.

"I guess we're all going, since it's kind of hard to play one-handed poker." Isaac stood and stretched. "Besides, with a bunch of horny women leaving the Ugly Stick, we might get lucky tonight."

"I've been in the middle of that mob before. Scared

the jitters out of me," Jackson admitted. "Let's go 'round the back to the front and find Greta Sue. She can run interference."

"She can't guard us all. Frankly, I don't want her to. I'll take my chances with the ladies." Isaac rubbed his hands together. "I could use a little distraction after having my butt kicked at poker."

"Must be the Jameson luck," Nick said.

Isaac chuckled. "Remind me not to play poker with Jackson and Nick. I'm completely out of my league here."

"We both are." Trent jerked his head toward the door. "Come on."

Jackson feathered through the handful of bills he collected from the table and stuffed them in his pocket. "You two are more than welcome to come throw money at us anytime."

Nick headed for his tow truck he'd parked at the rear of the building. Tonight was a full moon. People always got crazy at the full moon. Otherwise, the mechanic would have ridden his motorcycle.

Jackson climbed into the passenger seat of the tow truck's cab.

Trent and Isaac slowly walked around the building.

"Did you put that ad in the paper for a ranch hand?" Isaac asked.

Trent shook his head. "I put a flyer up at the feed store and here at the Ugly Stick."

"I took a whack at an ad for the newspaper, we'll see what we can get. We have more work than we can shake a stick at and no relief until Dusty gets back."

Dusty, their ranch foreman, was out recuperating from knee replacement after having been thrown one too many times by Thunder, the meanest horse they had.

"Yeah, cattle to round up, horses to train and pastures to cut. Should have hired someone a month ago."

"Whose idea was it anyway for us to do our own ranchin'? We have the money to pay someone else," Trent reminded Isaac.

"I can hear Dad's voice in my head. *You're gettin' too big for your britches, boy.*" Isaac dug his thumbs in his belt loops and rocked back on his boot heels with a deep scowl, just like their father wore when he was delivering a lecture on the sins of laziness. Isaac's frown turned around and he grinned.

Trent didn't. Their taciturn father had backhanded him more than once, and he'd sworn never to return to the Triple J Ranch outside of Temptation, Texas. He hadn't come back until he'd gotten news from his brother that Old John Jameson had died of a heart attack, leaving his two-thousand-acre spread to his boys.

If he'd had his way, Trent would have sold the ranch and given the proceeds to the Wounded Warriors organization or some other worthy cause. But Isaac hadn't wanted to give it up. He'd felt some sort of connection to the place.

Hell, he'd been their father's favorite and could do no wrong. The ranch probably held *good* memories for him.

Now they both lived there and worked the ranch with their own hands. Although Trent had never wanted to keep the ranch, he'd never been closer to his brother, and he was starting to work out his anger toward his father. But it was a struggle to keep the ranch going when he had full-time commitments as an oil rig architect. And the time spent ranching had given him a little more understanding and grudging respect for his late father.

Isaac had insisted they do the work themselves, telling him it would keep them humble when their bank accounts were overflowing and they could have anything they wanted.

Trent wasn't afraid of hard work, but they needed help to keep the ranch up. The fences alone took all their time, mending and restringing wire to keep the cattle from straying. And the horses needed exercise and training, and the hay needed cutting.

Sure, they had a foreman who ran the place when they were away on business, but even he needed help while they were gone. Now that Dusty was out for several months, they realized just how much he'd had on his plate.

Yeah, they could use an extra pair of hands and the sooner the better.

In the meantime, his younger brother still had great expectations of finding a woman to love.

Not Trent. As a twenty-year-old, he'd thought he was in love with an older woman in her late twenties, only to find out she'd been lying to him, cheating on him with a man who could afford to buy her jewelry and fancy dates.

Since then, he hadn't trusted a woman and never went past two dates with one, determined to keep them at a distance.

"You gonna help get the trucks out of the ditch?"

"I suppose." Trent glanced at Isaac. "Go on, see if you can rescue a damsel in distress from the perils of a rowdy Ladies Night at the Ugly Stick. I'm sure one would happily take you home to tuck her into bed." His thoughts returned to the sandy-blond-haired cowgirl who'd almost busted his nose. Some of his parts, besides his nose, still throbbed at her image seared in his mind.

She hadn't been the prettiest woman he'd ever seen, but she was definitely intriguing. He wondered if she'd ever found Audrey.

He also wondered if he'd see her again. Used to being chased by women, Trent found the trespasser more than intriguing, considering she was the first woman who hadn't been too interested in kissing him.

The competitive spirit in him had flagged her as a challenge, one he'd surely overcome and grow bored with once he had caught, kissed and bedded her.

ABOUT THE AUTHOR

Twenty years of livin' and lovin' on a South Texas ranch raising horses, cattle, goats, ostriches and emus left an indelible impression on Myla Jackson, one she likes to instill in her red-hot stories. Myla pens wildly sexy, fun adventures of all genres including historical westerns, medieval tales, romantic suspense, contemporary romance and paranormal beasties of all shapes and sexy sizes. She lives in the tree-covered hills of Northwest Arkansas with her husband of more than 20 years and her muses—the human-wanna-be canines—Chewy and Sweetpea.

To learn more about Myla Jackson and her alter ego Elle James visit:
www.mylajackson.com
mylajackson@mylajackson.com

Honor Bound

Duty Bound

River Bound

Paranormal

Shewolf

Thorn's Kiss

Sex, Lies & Vampire Hunters